AS THE TWIG IS BENT

AS THE TWIG IS BENT...

The tale of a young man in frontier Montana

Dorwin Schreuder

All Rights Reserved
April 2020
First Edition
IBSN:9781735580616
IBSN:

To my family and friends
who encouraged me to keep writing.

Table of Contents

PREFACE

Many came west to escape, perhaps from even themselves.

How many lie in graveyards beneath crudely marked stones and how many were left forgotten, across foothills and valleys beneath prairie grass?

I have traveled and lived in the territory where these fictitious characters only sixty years earlier, were acting in historical settings. It is remarkable that pioneers endured in the rugged land that even today will trample the life of all but the hardy.

As the railroad opened the Yellowstone Valley, the towns of Clermont and Coulson were replaced and renamed with Worden and Billings respectively. Huntley has retained its original riverside identity.

As you journey here, if you will, imagine and question, could this have really happened?

Dorwin Schreuder
Author

CHAPTER 1   DESPERATION

I was sick to my bones with the constant jostling of the horse drawn freight wagon. Worn to an aching vessel of bruised blood by the pounding of the bouncing wooden plank floor on which I lay, I longed for the site of our humble shelter-home, still a full day away. Pa had been driving the wagon for almost three days, since we left the little settlement of Coulson on the Yellowstone River in Montana Territory.

A cold breeze was invading the edges of the worn horse blanket wrapped around my thin body. Autumn was losing to winter, and Pa had given up. Without voice, his sagging shoulders and lack of movement spoke for his heart. He sat on the driver's bench ahead of me, staring northeast over the horses' backs into the vast distance between us and the Musselshell River, which lie so far ahead. As our direction wobbled around nature's barriers, we followed no wagon tracks, no charted path, not even a game trail. Only life's circumstances led us forward.

Ma and Pa came to Montana Territory from St. Louis in 1867, traveling most of the way by steamboat. Both had inherited a small amount of money from relatives with which they planned to purchase a few cattle and start a homestead ranch north of the Crow Indian Reservation, in what was called the Musselshell Basin. Neither had ever been here before. They had only read about it in a government newspaper advertisement. From the beginning, Pa never seemed to get control of anything. Ma was supportive, but in a way that supporting a falling tree will only get you crushed.

They built a small cabin at the edge of timbered land near the river. I came into the world unattended shortly after the cabin door was hung. Within a year, lightning ignited the timber and burned the cabin, along with a log barn, into a black pile of ash. With little to work with and no help, Pa was forced to make a home out of a partial cave he dug into the rocky hillside breaks further back from the river. The roof over our one room haven has been a weave of logs and brush...my only home of fourteen years, and is the destination to end this torturous wagon journey. Without a barn, most of the cattle either fell prey to wolves and grizzlies, were siphoned off by wandering bands of Crow or Piegan Indians, or died of exposure during the first harsh winter. But Pa was resilient until my little sister, Millie, was born, three years after me. He struggled to feed us, with a little farming, mostly withered by drought. Plagued with unending tragedies, and broken by poverty he resisted with steadfast faith that "tomorrow" would bring relief.

At age four my sister began losing weight and had little strength. Our nearest neighbor was twelve miles to the east and of little help, but Ma and Pa left me with them and took Millie to the nearest settlement thirty miles away, a place called Roundup, where there might be a doctor. Millie died there two days after arriving.

Ma was never quite the same after losing Millie. She was a strong person in body and in faith; tall with long brown hair and eyes that never quite let you inside her inner soul. She was often distant as if dreaming of some far away land, but happy to be both here and there. Then after Millie, much of the happiness faded. Pa recognized Ma's grief but kept struggling to make a life in the Musselshell wilderness. We lived off the land, eating elk, antelope, deer and fish. Most of the cattle we were able to save were traded for staples and dried food. The entire herd now numbered six.

When they journeyed into town, I didn't mind staying with the neighbors to the east. Chris and Anna Carlson had the only other child within miles; one child my age. Julie was a beautiful girl with the most wonderful smiling blue eyes and curly golden hair I had ever seen. We rarely saw each other more than three times a year but it was three more times than I ever saw any other girl, and I cherished every hour in her presence. When she talked to me, her soft voice made my stomach ache in a very different way than anything else. When she spoke, I sometimes pretended I couldn't hear her, discreetly approaching close enough to faintly feel the warmth of her breath. There was a magical fragrance in the path she walked. I worked to make every existing part of me perfect for her, but she always seemed to casually accept me just as I was; a tall blue eyed, sandy haired, wiry thin friend with great ambition.

Her parents were ranchers, but not as poor as us. Her Pa could afford to hire a couple hands who lived year-round in a room above the barn. Her Ma was pretty like Julie, and sometimes in the winter, took Julie with her to stay with an aunt somewhere in a place called Minnesota. Her Pa was nice too, but he occasionally hired a third hand that was terrible. His name was Morgan Marshall, but Julie and I called him "Mean Morgan." Mr. Carlson mostly hired Morgan to do mean things, like kill grizzlies, wolves, coyotes, and to scare away any other homesteaders who wanted to steal from him. Mean Morgan was ugly inside and out. Dirty hair hung from under his hat, and more covered his face. He wheezed from his big chest when he breathed out a foul smell, and he never smiled. It was frightening to even have him look at us.

One afternoon Julie and I were playing, building rock castles down by the creek, and we noticed "Mean Morgan" watching us from the brush on the other side. Julie whispered, "Mother told me to stay away from Morgan because she doesn't trust him. When I told mother I was afraid of him, she confided that she was too."

Whether present or far, Julie and I hid from the shadow of "Mean Morgan" in her infinite backyard.

In the spring of 1881 Ma and Pa went to Roundup for supplies. After I had spent a joyful four-day vacation with Julie and her parents, they returned with Ma not riding on the front bench seat. She was not feeling well. The two-day trip itself was usually enough to weaken her spirits so Pa and I worked to make her comfortable and rest. Ma was not a complainer, nor did she ever expect special attention. But she did not look well. A day later she came down with a terrible fever. Pa said people in the town had been sickened with what he called "scarlet fever." Ma lay in bed for four days, hardly breathing, her face and hands burning up with fever. Pa had to help her up and outside to relieve herself. Pa and I tried to keep her cool with rags soaked in water. I couldn't leave her side, because I rarely did anything without her. She knew she was fading because she told me she loved me, and admonished me to grow strong and learn to "do what is right." But after three days, she wasn't able to drink anything, her voice became very weak and she spoke of things that didn't make sense. I was holding her hand on the fifth day, when Ma died.

We buried her down by the creek where the old barn had burned. The earth was soft there and Ma used to like to sit nearby on a big mossy rock. I often saw her there among the wild flowers in the spring with her toes at the edge of the water, or at the first color of sunset, brushing her long brown hair. The trees were now growing back and Pa had promised to rebuild the barn there as soon as a few more of the trees had grown strong enough. A cross chiseled into her sandstone throne marks where she rests.

I was fourteen and I had seen things die, but not Ma. She was my everything. I knew she was missing something inside that makes us keep believing. I knew she was tired. But how could she leave me? I couldn't accept it, and for two days I was unable to eat. I cried until my face was crusted with salt and dirt. Pa was no better, and rarely spoke to me. I understand now that he couldn't find worthwhile words either.

I finally cried myself back into reality. Afterwards, Pa and I confusingly discussed our future. He was finally thinking of leaving the Musselshell Basin but had no idea where to go or what to do. The discussion only accented our despair and reached no conclusion. I suggested we report our fate to the Carlsons, because I ached for the empathy of Julie and the warmth of a soul I could feel. I convinced Pa I should saddle Old Billie and ride over at sunrise. Wanting to be alone with his grief, Pa agreed, but admonished me to be home before dark.

Old Billy was a draft horse, unaccustomed to our worn misshaped saddle, and his pace was not fast. I coaxed him into making the trip in three hours. Arriving at the Carlson's, I was surprised to see several saddled horses tied near the cabins and in the corral. When no one greeted me, I shyly approached the door, rehearsing the news I was about to provide Mrs. Carlson.

The weary mother of my best friend appeared and inquired, "Why Toby! How did you know?"

"Know what?" I blurted.

"Julie's missing!"

I fell silent. I stared in disbelief. When I could breathe again, I asked, "From where, when, how long, why?"

She explained that two days ago Julie had walked up to the bluffs about half a mile from the cabin intent on fossil hunting; her favorite kind of outing. She left alone about midafternoon, and never returned. Word was spreading throughout the Basin and friends were arriving to help with the search. Her fossil basket had been found at the edge of the bluff trail, but nothing else had been located.

It was a time when words were no use at all. I rudely stumbled from the cabin to Old Billy and guided him to the secret places Julie and I shared. Each little pool, every shady bank, all the "secret" fossil beds. I found nothing. Something must have carried her away. Something awful! I could not allow myself to imagine the horror. Before Ma died, during one of her Bible teaching sessions, she attempted to explain hell, and I didn't understand the concept. Now it was all becoming clear. Hell could descend upon you without the presence of fire.

I don't even remember the ride back home. In the saddle, I just turned Old Billy loose and he knew the way. Arriving at dusk I tended to Old Billy and entered the shelter. Pa could tell something was very wrong. He broke the silence.

"What is it?"

"She's gone."

CHAPTER 2   HEADING OUT

Then it was just Pa and me. There wasn't anything left for him; as his dreams had all become nightmares. I was his pal, but not really. Pa was not a talker. I couldn't help him with grown up things, nor talk with him about what we should do next. He had nobody in St. Louis where he had come from, and even if he did, his pride wouldn't let him go back. I was only fourteen, but I realized that Pa too, was sick. He desperately needed something to mend his mind and heal his spirits. He at times mentioned joining the search for gold a hundred miles or so to the west, but knew the venture was even more of a risk than his attempt at ranching.

Ma home schooled me in both regular school subjects and Bible studies. Our most frequently read book was a large Bible she brought from St. Louis, and somehow saved from the cabin destroying forest fire. She always taught me if I prayed unselfishly for something, God would give my wishes serious consideration. I prayed for Pa, myself, and Julie, until one day two drovers passed through our lower pasture with a small herd of cattle. They stopped and talked with Pa and me and told us about the

Northern Pacific Railroad being built up through the Yellowstone Valley. According to the drovers the rails were following the river and plans were to go all the way to the end of the Bozeman trail and maybe "clear to the ocean." The drovers had come from near Miles City but were considering selling their cattle at Roundup and getting a job with the railroad.

The butts of their horses hadn't disappeared over the hill when I saw Pa's expression begin to change. I asked, "Do you think I could get a job on the railroad too?"

He said, "Well, maybe. They might need a water boy. You want to take a trip down there and see if we can get on?"

I saw new life in him, and said, "Sure, when can we go?"

His reply didn't take long. "The drovers said the tracks are about to a place along the Yellowstone they call Clermont, about twenty miles east of another trading place they call Coulson. We'll have to cross the Yellowstone near the big rock that Lewis and Clark named Pompey's Pillar. There's a break in the cliffs there and the river is shallow enough in the fall to cross. We can get supplies either at Clermont or Coulson. If we can get on, we'll come back and take the remaining six steers to Roundup and use the money to outfit us for the railroad."

Pa had apparently thought all this through in a matter of just minutes. I was not wanting to change his mind, but was hesitant to embark on such a journey without considerable preparation.

It was going to be a forty-mile ride one way, in a freight wagon because we had to bring back supplies in case we didn't get hired. Another good reason for the freight wagon was it was all we had. We didn't have a buggy. The wagon was only mid-sized, but was old and heavy. It should be drawn by four horses instead of two, but "Old Billy" and "Canker" were all we had. They would be slow and had to be rested often. We could not expect to make more than twenty miles in a long day, even over good terrain.

We had very little to lose; return or not. The cattle were on open range. They wouldn't wander far. Weathered and sagging, our only door had no lock. Three walls of the shelter were sandstone and the other was rotting logs. If a wandering saddle tramp came by, he could do no harm sheltering for the night. Wagon tools, harness repairs, dried meat, beans and biscuits were put in the wagon along with a ground canvass and blankets.

Pa reminded me to take my winter coat because fall colors were beginning to show and, "You know how quick the weather can change here in Montana Territory." Pa put his rifle under the wagon seat saying, "I don't expect no trouble, but we will be traveling through the Crow reservation and I hear they are not too happy about the railroad."

We left at sunrise in late September. Pa thought we could make the banks of the Yellowstone by Pompey's Pillar in two days. We could cross at daylight on the third day and make it to the rail office at Clermont by noon.

The trip was fun, at first. It was beautiful fall weather, dry and sunny. I had never been more than 20 miles away from our humble home. My only travels were with Pa on hunting trips. Those trips were my survival classrooms. He taught me how to track and to shoot, saying that he had learned the hard way. By that he meant his knowledge came like everything else he experienced; by trial, error, and frequent failure.

On the first afternoon, I shot a prairie chicken while I was riding on the wagon seat. I skinned it by myself, and we cooked it over a sagebrush fire at day's end. That night we slept in the wagon bed with millions of stars watching over us. It was cold, but as I looked up, I was sure that God was considering my requests. And I still kept one request constant. I hoped that somehow Julie was still alive.

By the end of the second day, our backs were sore from the endless twisting and lurching of the wagon wheels making their own trail over the bunch grass and cactus. The horses were needing to rest more often. Pa thought he found the trail that would lead to the river crossing, but it led to a small rock quarry instead. We were still high above the river with 300-foot sandstone cliffs separating us from the riverbed. From the rim of the cliffs, looking down onto the river, we could see the Pompey's Pillar rock about half a mile to the west. We bounced along the rim until we located a break in the rocks that led us down through a wide wash to a group of cottonwood trees at the river's edge. It was late in the day; the horses were exhausted so we made camp among the cottonwoods. However, the night was not so pleasant as before due to clouds of mosquitos feeding on any exposed flesh. The high-pitched droning of their countless miniature wings competed with the pulsing chirp of nearly as many unseen crickets to maintain a tireless chorus throughout the night.

As we lay there listening to natures symphony, Pa told me the history of the curious rock formation directly across the river from us. It was a large sandstone structure, hundreds of feet in circumference, towering two hundred feet above the river's flood plain. It was named Pompey's Tower by the famous explorer William Clark who led the Lewis and Clark expedition to explore this area. On his way returning to the settled part of the United States, William Clark carved his name in the wall of the sandstone on July 25, 1806. The exploration party camped nearby and Clark wrote in his journal that the many bison in the area made so much noise, they were kept awake. I thought it sad that we were probably camped in nearly the same place, but in only a little more than seventy years all the bison had been killed and replaced with mosquitos. I covered my head with the horse blanket and wondered what a railroad looked like.

The next morning, we set out to cross the river. A shallow gravel bar rested diagonally across three fourths of the flow with only a narrow passage of dark swiftly running water hiding its depth. Pa cut a long willow pole from a thicket and determined after several probes the passage had a gentle slope and could be waded by both him and the horses. It appeared that others had gone the same way in the recent past.

Pa put a short rope on Old Billy's bridle. I sat in the wagon seat reining the horses while Pa probed the passage with the pole in one hand and Old Billy's tether in the other. Canker objected to water up to his belly but Pa and Billy pulled him through. The crossing went without incident. We were on the south side of the Yellowstone; Pompey's rock was to our left and our next task was to find the railroad.

The valley near the big rock was narrow enough to be able to see from the river cliffs to the foothills on the other side. We saw no railroad. It appeared that the drover's story was a little ahead of reality. We drove the wagon to the middle of the valley where we finally recognized what appeared to be preliminary surveying activity. Although we knew the tracks were supposed to be advancing from the east, it appeared that brush piles were stacked off in the distance to the west. Pa hastened Canker and Old Billy toward the brush piles.

As we passed the huge mounds of uprooted sage and dry greasewood brush, additional grading scars assured us we were following the beginning of a new railroad bed. Finally, a dust cloud to the west led us to a group of sweating men pulling sage from the ground with chains hitched to some of the largest horses I ever saw. Pa pulled our team up to a big burly man directing the operation and inquired about work.

"Looks like you have a good crew here, but if I wanted to join the group how would I sign on?"

The boss replied as if he was dissatisfied with his own answer, "I don't do no hiring here. Most of that's done up in Coulson. That's upriver about thirty miles."

Pa, unhappy with the response asked, "What's the best way to get there?"

Pointing to the west the boss said, "You'll find the stage trail that comes from Miles City crosses the valley just ahead. Go west a couple miles to Clermont. There ain't nothing much there but our supplies and a couple of our tents. Keep on a-goin' till you get to Huntley. There's nobody there that knows anything either, but there's a post office and a store. The old boy that runs the store also runs the ferry ta gitcha 'cross the river. Take it 'cause there ain't no other place to cross for miles. From Huntley it's about eighteen miles to where Coulson's built there in what they call 'Clarks Fork Bottom' of the Yellowstone. We got a railroad office there."

We arrived at Clermont in less than an hour. It was a small cluster of buildings that appeared to be built mostly to serve the coming railroad. We watered the horses and moved on.

Pa was beginning to get discouraged, although the grading boss said there would be many men hired in the next few weeks. Pa had been driving the horses pretty hard and, in another hour, we clanked into Huntley. Pa had very little money to spare, but he bargained with a local trader for just enough food to briefly break the boredom of our dried meat; and paid for our ferry ride across the river.

Huntly was laid out close to the river. The ferry crossing was made with a flat barge tied to ropes anchored on each side of the river. We were thankful for the ferry, because the current was strong, and the channel deep.

We struck out for Coulson, twenty miles to the west. Old Billy and Canker were worn out. We found a low "flat" near the river where there was still grass for their feed, and shade for our rest. That evening we slept under the wagon to avoid a cold autumn shower. Hungry coyotes slinking through the brush disturbed the horses and again kept us awake most of the night.

Early the next morning Old Billy and Canker were straining against their traces and the rattling wagon was again rolling west. The sun was showing midday when we found the railroad office in the muddy raucous little town of Coulson. I had never seen so many buildings and people in one place in my life. There was something close to twenty buildings with finished roofs, and several more under construction. There must have been thirty people in an around the edges of town. They seemed to be concentrated near one of the larger buildings with a high flat store front bearing the sign, *"Headquarters-wines, liquors, cigars."* With great anticipation I trailed behind Pa into the building, labeled "Northern Pacific Railway." Inside, Pa looked toward a desk where a trio of men were leaving. One large nail into the desk side held a sign, "Employment."

A ruddy, pulpy faced short man at the desk looked at us for a moment. He seemed to be eating an unlit cigar, which left a thin brown ring of dried slobber around his mouth. As he sat back in his chair, his belly covered his belt. His bushy eyebrows held on to tiny flakes of dry skin having departed his block shaped forehead, all suffering between two tufts of protruding ear hair.

He inquired in an unfriendly voice. "And what can I do for you?"

Pa answered loud and confident, "We want to work for the railroad."

Looking at me, the clerk asked, "And him?"

Pa took a deep breath and replied, "He's a strong boy."

The railroad man sat back in his chair, his belly peeking through a missing button on his wrinkled shirt. He hesitated, and picked up a pencil. Reaching for a pad he asked, "OK, what's your name."

"Alex, ah, Alexander Hawthorn."

"And his?"

I chimed in with, "Tobias Hawthorn. Pa calls me Toby"

"Where do you live?"

Pa took over again, "In the Musselshell Basin."

The man looked up from the pad and said, "No, I mean where around here do you live?"

This caught Pa by surprise. He hesitatingly explained, "We just got here. It's been a four-day trip."

"Well then where or how do you want me to contact you when or if we decide to hire you?"

Pa breathed deeply and said, "I understood you were hiring right away. Look, I can go to work tomorrow, or this afternoon, as soon as I find a place to park my wagon."

The puffy old clerk removed his cigar stub and placed it on the stained desk. With cold indifference he said, "Look mister. See this tablet. It's full of men who want a job. Everybody gets in the book, goes on a list, waits their turn. And their turn comes when the rails and the ties get here from the saw mill or the east. Now they're supposed to be here, but they ain't. And I don't know when they'll get here, but maybe not for some weeks yet. The Missouri ain't bridged and they're have'n trouble get'n started. Barges are slow. They usually come up with the work train. So if'in you and the kid want a job you best come in and check the list every couple of days. I keep every name for only one week and toss it cause there's plenty of names and plenty of no-show drifters. I put the names that are drawn for jobs up on the wall over there and if there are no shows we just get more from the list. Yuh got a friend that can check for yuh fine; otherwise you'll be off the wall in one week. Yuh can come back and apply again, but the best chance of gittin on is when the track is gittin built right here."

Pa looked pale. His lips pursed and in a quivering voice said, "We've come a long way. There's not much left of what we use to be. Can't you make an exception?"

Closing the tablet, the railroad man answered, "It ain't my job to take care of people. I have to explain this to dozens of people every day. Don't ask me to do it again."

Pa walked past several buildings back to the store where several of the men were standing around outside and asked, "Are you men waiting to get hired by the railroad?" Most of them nodded a yes. Then Pa asked, "How long have you been waiting?"

One of the men answered, "Most of us been a-waiten nigh on two weeks."

As Pa loaded what supplies he could afford into the wagon, there was nothing to discuss. We departed with him providing a one sentence explanation. "We can't stay here indefinitely."

CHAPTER 3   THE RETURN

As I lay on the wagon floor with nothing to do but tolerate the pounding from the rough terrain, my disordered mind churned through our decisions, causing me to question. In a half-conscious daze, I pondered:

Why didn't Pa take a known, or marked trail north out of Coulson to Roundup, and then east to the Musselshell Basin and our homestead? We never intended to travel as far up the Yellowstone as Coulson or the nearby settlement they are calling Billings, but Pa was desperate to lay aside our past and bring us new life. Now with winter threatening, his desperation is reversed, he is choosing to drive the horses in a direct line northeast back home toward Rattlesnake Buttes and the Musselshell River.

Pa had mentioned that if we go by the way the crow flies, we can save two days travel. I'm no longer confident he knows exactly where we are, or where we're going. The crow flies over the vertical walls of sandstone, and around the tall timbered buttes. We must zigzag our way through them. Several dry creeks were easily navigated leaving the horses to suffer between water sources. Pa finally says he recognizes the territory from prior hunting trips, but our trip has now been extended at least two days.

I'm strong enough to drive the horses myself and should rest Pa, but with no trail to follow he has to sit up front to pick a safe route through the rough terrain. I'm here passing hours resting my back on the wagon floor, or watching the parched terrain scratch past the side boards. Season ending colors are fading to drab shades of bleached grass and patches of blue grey sage, all clinging to cracked earth polygons, serving as an anchor against the wind. Only the pines and scrub junipers of the foothills are adding variety to the color of desolation.

As I lay here on old splintering grey boards, fear is creeping into my stomach. The wagon wheels are old. The steel rimmed edges are forced fit over oak quarter sawn wedges and spokes that are withered, dried and shrunken to where they no longer fit tight. Only makeshift wire clamps hold some of them in place. All the while our torturous "shortcut" is showing no mercy for the aging wagon.

The longer my contemplation the more fear and anxiety plague my every thought. The hollowness of Pa's last plea to the railroad clerk keeps tracking through my mind. *"There's not much left of what we used to be."* What is left? How long does nothing last? Shall we wither away, become mindless eating wild meat in a rock walled dugout for another winter, only to see spring bring fresh flowers to die among? Pa seems to have no plan. I'll soon be 15, yet he fails to discuss our plight with me as if I were a child needing coddling. I have never been to a real school, but Ma made me read from the Bible, the dictionary, and write letters to imaginary people, which of course we never mailed. At an early age I began to understand what was happening to us, more so what was not happening and asked about the rest of the world. Wistfully, Ma always said I must be patient and life would be thrust upon me when I was ready.

Pa has never adjusted to the west. He and Ma lived a good life in St. Louis. Pa was something called a land broker. Ma operated a fancy-dress shop, even wearing some of her finest to Montana Territory. Their occupations were earned, but yet were handed down to them through their families. When they were married, neither family approved of their marriage. Each side had come from different parts of Europe and believed in contrasting religions. To escape the conflict, they indulged in the advertised fantasy of going west and becoming rich off of free land. They expected to turn cattle loose and have them multiply as rabbits on the prairie and to have wheat waving abundantly in the mountain foothills. But within a few seasons, reality silenced the siren's rumor. All was lost, yet both were too proud to return to their roots in humility. In their hearts both wanted to surrender. They realized they had not the knowledge or means to continue in the harsh world they blindly rushed into to tame; but neither soul would bow before the other. They could not join together in their failure. Both wanted something unreachable, beyond their grasp, because simply surviving consumed their every effort. They labored only in the present, unable to develop a truthful vision of their fate. Now Pa, with no plan, was still trying to hang on. He is no longer imagining tomorrow, and is barely seeing today.

In thought, I returned from where I was and shivered from a brisk gust of wind. It was late afternoon and the new wind foretold a change in weather. I sat upright to watch the "dust devils" rise out of the sage and swirl among the sandstone boulders. As I watched the display, a wagon wheel sized tumble weed, bearing a foot-long stick in its roots rolled at gale speed directly at Canker's chest. The stick hit the old horse in the neck while the giant weed lodged on the wagon pole between Canker and Old Billy. Both horses spooked into a terror-stricken run. Pa, caught by surprise, lost grip of Canker's line, braced his feet and began yelling "Whoa" while pulling on Old Billy's lead. I tried to move forward to help, but the wagon was bouncing so badly with the contents slamming against my legs that I made no progress. Pa shouted for me to jump. I lurched for the seat just as Old Billy dodged the opposite direction to avoid a large rock. My stomach hit the side board and I somersaulted into the brush below. Twenty yards further the right front wheel struck a boulder half as tall as the axle, broke it at the hub and sent the wheel rolling off downhill. With the horses still running at full speed the iron axle dug into the ground plowing a furrow until it hit another rock. The axle stopped abruptly, but the wagon did not. The entire wagon vaulted over the rock, flipped upside down and broke apart. The pole and wagon tongue broke away from the wagon and the horses continued to run over the rise ahead and out of sight.

I couldn't see Pa. The skyward wheels of the wagon were still turning when I got to the wreckage. I called for Pa but there was no answer. When I reached what remained of the wagon front, I immediately knew. . . I was now totally alone.

Pa had been thrown forward when the plowing axle hit the rock. He must have landed outstretched on the ground, but the wagon flipped over on top of him, and slid, making his upper body almost unrecognizable.

I stepped back from the scene, unable to look closely at Pa's fate. My fear was gone. All of my senses were icily calm. I was not grief stricken, but most likely in shock. Somehow, I anticipated something like this would happen before we returned to the Musselshell. I now had to think for myself, and only myself. From this day forward I must have a plan.

In deep dread I thought, "The last years of Ma and Pa were hard. It seemed all too easy for them to die. It is going to be much harder for me to live."

CHAPTER 4   FINDING SHELTER

It was late in the day. The weather was changing for the worse. But the first thing I had to do was bury Pa. I salvaged an old shovel out of the wreckage and surveyed the ground where my present life was now scattered. A small rise among the rocks ten yards safely uphill seemed a peaceful place for Pa. From there Pa could see down a valley and to the buttes to the west. The afternoon view would prepare him for the sunsets he so loved. I dug a shallow grave and lay him in it. But before I completed the sorrowful task, I began to think about myself. What do I do next? I must survive from here. Pa's coat was better than mine. It was too big, but much warmer because I had outgrown my own. And what about his boots? He had just purchased new ones in anticipation of working on the railroad, and again my own were causing blisters, too small and worn through at the soles. He was without his hat which had separated during his fall. Could I be so heartless as to take my own father's clothes before I bury him?

I stumbled away. This time I fell to the earth and cried. To be so alone, so desperate, so uncertain cannot be described by any, even those who may have survived it. In time the cold wind brought me to my senses. I reasoned that Pa would want me to take all that I could. I removed the clothing from his stiffening limbs without a further tear, gaining strength as I worked. With my own discarded coat covering his disfigured body, I drug him into the depression and positioned him with respect, hands folded across his chest. I pushed most of the dirt back into place but was unable to console myself enough to pack it down over Pa. Instead I placed large rocks over the grave and spread the remaining dirt in the voids to seal out the rest of nature. I considered making a grave marker with splintered wagon boards but thought Pa would never want to be an attraction, and certainly not to the prairie inhabitants.

As I finished the sun was setting. I knew it was unsafe to travel in the dark, and I didn't even know which direction I should choose. I constructed a makeshift shelter from the wind out of parts of the wagon and prepared to stay for the night. Perhaps I could find the horses in the morning.

I lay awake most of the night, breathing with the wind, occasionally convulsing with hiccup-like sobs. It was so very dark. Low level clouds eliminated stars, moon and any sense of light. The depts of the darkness coached me into a pit of pity that I lay in until the first glimmer of light sent both relief and new fear over the pine crested bluffs. The morning greeted me like a hungry dragon.

I rose, folded my blanket and stowed any loose supplies under the largest remaining part of the wagon. I picked up Pa's wide brimmed hat and stood tall under it. I braced for the day thinking, "This is the first day of the rest of my life, and I'm not going to waste even two breaths of it." I thought of Ma and the 23rd Psalm, repeated it in my mind, but when recalling the words, *I fear no evil,* they fell weakly upon me. I conceded, "I am afraid out here all alone." I set out to find the horses.

Their trail was easy to follow. They were at a full gallop dragging the wagon pole and parts of the hitch. Not more than a hundred yards ahead, over a small hill I saw them lying together at the base of a half dead pine tree. They appeared to have run into the man-sized trunk, one on each side while still hooked together by the harness.

The scene was horrible. Old Billy was facing south opposite of Canker who fell looking north, the stump upright between them. Old Billy had opened his gut on a lower broken dry branch and had been dead for several hours. Canker appeared to have tumbled forward in the harness and broke his neck, but was still breathing, struggling very slowly. Reaching in my pocket I took the knife Pa told me always to carry, and cut away the leather traces in the longest lengths available. I realized it would not be possible to save Canker. I needed to put him to rest here with his partner without further suffering. So alone, I began to speak to myself.

"Is there no end to the death I must witness. This knife can kill this poor horse, but how can I be the one who guides it to its mark? God has this blood on his hands. None of it is on mine. Yet I must do old Canker the favor of ending his misery. I should have brought Pa's rifle with me. A bullet is so much less personal."

Just as I was about to turn back for the rifle, Canker shuddered his last breath. I stood over them both, pondering the enormity of what should be done. The gift of memory brought me the sound of Ma's voice from a Bible passage, "From dust to dust", and something additional that meant in time we all come and go and nature takes care of it.

I drug the leather harness pieces back to the wagon wreck and realized I buried Pa without a word. I walked to the arrangement of stones and stood there wondering what to say to Pa, who so seldom replied anyway. I remembered a poem from a book Ma had me read. I recited it to Pa and the morning wind.

"If I knew you and you knew me –

I'm sure that we would differ less,

And clasp our hands in friendliness,

If I knew you and you knew me."

Pa liked to have Ma and me sing to him and his favorite hymn came to mind. It wouldn't sound the same without Ma, but I tried with the words:

"Abide with me, fast falls the even-tide;

The darkness deepens; Lord, with me abide"

It wasn't the same without Ma, and I couldn't finish it. Pa was dead and I was only making myself feel worse. I said what Ma often said at the end of Hymns. "The Lord be with You."

Having said my last goodbyes, I turned from the grave, never to look back.

I had some decisions to make. I was alone, so very alone, and I had nowhere to go.

CHAPTER 5   ROOM MATES

The storm bearing down upon me put an urgency in every movement. I knew that to stay here in the open valley would be sure death from exposure. My best estimate for shelter from the wind and most likely snow would be from the low mountains about two miles to the west. Pa mentioned there were caves and mines in the bluffs, and I could see huge rocks and sandstone cliffs from where I stood. I thought to carry as much as possible, but that would not be enough to survive for long. The grass was long enough to allow sliding over it, presenting the idea of constructing a two board drag with wagon pieces and harness lines. It didn't look as good as the ones Indians used but it worked. I strapped on food, a few tools for shelter building, Pa's rifle and ammunition, a tarp and blankets and various other things Pa had thought necessary for our winter in Musselshell. As a last thought, I parceled out a portion of a bag of salt, thinking it may be good for curing meat. After pulling the drag for no more than 50 yards, I decided to stow a third of it back in the overturned wagon and return for it later. I began trudging the longest two miles in Montana Territory. After an hour of exertion, I was sweating even in the cold wind out of the approaching storm. I foolishly had brought no water but I had two empty buckets containing various tools. Empty buckets were no consolation with no water in sight.

A half mile from the nearest of the large rock cliffs, sleet started pelting my body, bouncing off the ground and stinging my face. Within seconds I was reaching for Pa's bigger coat. I was already wearing his wide brimmed hat which kept the sleet, soon turned to snow, off my face.

The wind did not bring the snow slowly. It advanced in a solid wall of white. If I didn't concentrate on the rocks ahead, I could easily stagger in circles; yet looking forward into the horizontal snow stole all warmth from my face, causing a severe pain deep in my upper skull. I could only endure short glances to maintain my direction. The snow made pulling the drag a little easier, but only until it began to deepen and Pa's boots slid on the wet prairie hill. My leg muscles where cramping when I finally reached the first boulder. I sat on the lee side, now feeling the chill of a new winter. Even while sheltered by the boulder, the snow was covering me relentlessly.

When the first snow squall subsided, I could see more of my surroundings. Above me were large rock slides sprinkled with long needled pines and assorted boulders of infinite sizes. It was still snowing but I could not afford to delay finding a place to shelter. I left my supplies and began scaling the bluffs.

I reached a lesser incline caused by scree accumulating behind a giant boulder. A tree grew next to the boulder and leaned crookedly into the vertical cliff only 5 feet away. The climb had been steep and my lungs were gasping for air. I sat there resting briefly when I caught a quick glimpse of movement near the tree. A large black wolf was peering at me through the lower branches of the pine. I didn't move until he soon turned and vanished.

But where did he go? I cautiously crawled to where he was spying on me. "Thank you, Lord, for bringing me the snow." Because of it I could see his tracks; under another tree, around a fallen log and between an opening in the rocks. Crawling further I could see that "Wolf" had disappeared into a cave.

I retreated to my pack as the snow again began defining a Montana blizzard. I pulled the entire pack up the rock slide with me, fearing that if the snow covered it, I may not find it for days. Approaching the cave, I began wondering how I was going to convince Wolf to share his home with me. Perhaps he would enjoy dining with me, if I was the meal. I untied Pa's...no, now my rifle, checked the load, and crawled to the opening. The contrast between the inner darkness and the snow left me sightless as I peered in. I could see nothing at first but could feel a faint draft of warm air coming from within; meaning the cave had depth and hopefully size. I lay there with my head and shoulders part way through the opening, rifle pointing into the darkness, half expecting Wolf to remove my scalp. But nothing happened. I slithered a little deeper. Still nothing happened. I began to see significant depth beyond me with shadows and spears of light from the opening behind me. I rolled far enough that I could sit up, and my eyes began to adjust to a cavern larger than in which I was raised. I did not see Wolf, yet I was sure he entered. Already we had something in common. A mutual threat to our well-being.

As I sat there scanning the dimness I thought, "It would help if Wolf wasn't so black." I listened. "Surely he must be panting back there somewhere behind a rock. Wait a minute dummy, it's winter, dogs and wolves don't pant much in their winter coats."

But I heard something else. Water dripping. There was no water running out of the cave opening, but it must be running down into the cave. My thirst came back, and my fear parched mouth barely fit around my swollen tongue. Yet I sat still, rifle in hand, needing to meet my landlord.

Eyesight adjusted; I could see the cave was divided into two levels just beyond the entrance. I had crawled to the lower level. The upper level rose to the right five feet above the entrance and terminated as a sandy platform protected by a guardrail of rocks. I also was sitting on an almost flat sandy surface vanishing toward a passage to the rear apparently leading deeper into the hillside. As I sat there glancing between the deeper tunnel and the upper platform, I saw him in the form of just two green eyes. He was watching me, perhaps from the instant I crawled into his den. We were thirty feet apart, but he kept his place and watched. He was lying on the sandy platform above me, mostly concealed by the rock ledge. I could have shot him, square between those two green eyes. But I wanted no more of death. If he would agree to my existence, I would agree to his. I had no idea how we would negotiate that agreement with any confidence. But I had no desire to harm anything.

After what must have been a patient hour of watching I realized that my pack was still out in the weather, soon to be buried with snow. I passed the first test with Wolf, I now had to see if he allowed furniture.

I crawled very slowly toward the cave opening, rifle still firmly in my grip. Wolf sat frozen as not to give away his position. Viewing from the outside, I could see the pole pack would barely slide through the opening without dismantling; allowing me to push it through ahead of me. Successfully inside with eyes adjusted, I had a new worry. Wolf was again no longer in sight. Assuming he was satisfied with remaining on his side of the cavern, I quietly sorted my worldly belongings, stopping with the dried food. I thought, "What wolf wouldn't like dried meat? Would he kill to get it? Probably, but will he want to kill me first; I'm not dried. But I will be if I don't get some water soon."

Forgetting about the meat for a moment, I took one of the buckets and filled it with snow from beside the cave opening. When I re-entered, Wolf had returned. He apparently found the spectacle of me entertaining and curious.

My attention turned again to the meat. I lashed the meat to one of the drag poles and propped it up on end against the cavern wall. It was seven feet above me, and still well below the jagged roof. I braced the stash with the second pole, and saw that Wolf was still watching me. He would have to be very brave to take anything from me. But what would become of me sleeping, or of my "room" in my absence. I certainly could not sit here in the dim light all winter. I thought the matter through in detail and reasoned that I must rest and study Wolf very carefully before placing any trust in him. I'm sure he was thinking the same.

Finally, the draft from below melted enough of the captured snow to begin sipping small swallows of ice water. The event was more rewarding than just providing water. It meant the rising air temperature was significantly above freezing. Wolf was becoming a good provider.

Not wanting to create anxiety in my companion, I settled against the rock wall on my side of the ample space and observed Wolf. He seemed content to do the same, looking undistracted in my direction. After what seemed like an hour had passed, watching and slowly hydrating myself with snow melt, I began to feel the call of nature of another sort. This began my first serious thoughts about wolf psychology. If I peed in the cave, would he be offended? I knew that dogs, coyotes and wolves marked their territory with their urine, and this was his territory. I was only attempting to become his guest. I did not want to appear to be aggressive.

As if Wolf was aware of my thoughts, he rose, stretched and cautiously walked to the opening and out into the storm. I moved so that I could observe him. He braced himself against the wind driven snow, stood on three legs, and peed on the trunk of the tree shadowing the opening. He did the same on the nearby rock and trotted out of sight. I wanted to follow him, but thought I should be here when he returned. I decided to bear the pressure a little longer so that I didn't invite him to invade my quarter of the cavern in my absence.

I had not to wait long. Wolf returned through the opening, shook himself violently, flicking snow over the entire entrance. He looked in my direction and proceeded to his perch with more confidence as if to say, "Oh, are you still here?"

That did it. Now I had to go, but I was not going to insult his housekeeping, or make my mark to compete with his. I put my face into the wind and walked a full ten yards from the entrance. The brief walk allowed me to stretch and observe my surroundings. However, I could see very little, and being unfamiliar with the terrain, risked getting lost from the cave. I retreated, brushed off the snow, and sat back to worry about how long the storm would last.

It appeared I had more food than Wolf, a worrisome condition not knowing his temperament. Light was fading. It was going to be a long very dark night. I knew I would not be able to venture out into the dark, and doubted Wolf would venture far in the storm. The prairie was a living pantry of food, both for Wolf and me. I had observed numerous rabbits, prairie dogs, sage hens, prairie chickens, deer and other smaller animals. But in this storm, none of them would be out exposed. All life would be surviving under cover. And the greatest immediate risk was that I was exhausted and had to sleep.

Wolf was smart. Long before me, he had made his bed on the upper ledge of the cave, so he could look down on the opening. Before he laid down, he circled at least twice padding the sand beneath him, and always laying with his head and view toward the entrance. He could remain invisible until the entering eye could adjusted to the dimness and look upward. I had to do even better.

I made my bed in the left corner of the cavern, in the sand. I placed all of my supplies behind me next to the stone wall. I smoothed the sand in front of me so that if I survived the night, I could tell if Wolf had snuck up close, exploring his chances during the night. For extra assurance I withdrew a roll of cord from Pa's…ah, again, MY mending supplies, and strung it across the area in front of me. With one end of the line taut to a rock and the other tied to my hat perched on a rock above me, I had an alarm that would fall and wake me if Wolf tripped over the line. For a final assurance, I wrapped myself completely, head and face included, in the horse blanket. If Wolf attacked, he would have to make his initial bite through the blanket and I would have a better chance to use the rifle. The wind was still howling when I began losing consciousness.

I awoke sometime well into the night believing I heard movement, but felt nothing near me. I froze scarcely breathing, but could see nothing. Perhaps it was Wolf going out to check the weather again, but it seemed to be slightly more. I strained to hear or see more, but all was still. What a feeling to be a stranger in a hostile world.

CHAPTER 6 USEFUL EDUCATION

Partly rested, my mind began to assess the reality of this new world:

"I am someplace between the Musselshell and Yellowstone Rivers, a north, south distance of around 40 miles, and maybe twenty miles east of the railroad town of Coulson. Nobody knows where I am, or even that I exist, except that little bit of ink on that puffy old railroad clerk's tablet. For sure he doesn't care about anything and in a few days not even my name will exist there. I have about three or four days of dried meat with me, and a little flour, salt and sugar plus some dried berries, potatoes and apples in a wrecked wagon two miles away. A few more things in the wagon would help keep me dry and cook some wild meat. I could cut meat off the horses. They'd be frozen stiff by now, but I'm sure I can shoot something much closer than two miles away. Besides, I don't think I could swallow any part of Canker or Old Billy. By morning the snow will be up over my boots, so that I can't walk to the wagon without freezing my feet, and even if I could wrap the boot tops I probably would 'post hole' into the drifted snow and could break a leg. With the loose snow the wind could come up and bury me or cause me to dig a snow cave; a situation much worse than staying here. I don't have any place I need to be real soon, and at least I am safe here for a while; that's if Wolf continues to eat outside of the cave. It's best I stay here and think this through."

"This storm can't last forever. What do I do when it quits? I have to feed myself. Maybe if I throw a little meat to Wolf, he will get to trust me better. I have to find something to shoot first. How long should I stay here? Where should I go? Not back to the homestead! There's nothing there for me. If I die right here in this cave, I will have accomplished more than if I went back there. I could look forward to being carried off by a mountain lion like Julie probably was. I can't go back there. I have nowhere to go, but I won't go back there. The only direction that makes sense is to head back south. If I can get to the Yellowstone, I can find the railroad and Coulson, and maybe the nearby town they are naming Billings. But how far is that? Can I walk that far? How long will it take? I probably can go afoot but it will have to be in good weather, and I will have to find food and water along the way. So, I can't go for several days. I have to think this through. I can't strike out like Pa without a plan. I have time, and I will be careful and wait until the time is right."

"But I gotta figure direction and distance! I remember that the gullies and dry creek beds right here seem to run to the south. That would mean I am still in the Yellowstone watershed, and not in the Missouri or Musselshell Buttes. If I followed a creek or some drainage, it should eventually lead me to the Yellowstone, although I paid attention during my trip with Pa, and we drove pretty much straight south. I'll wait till the sun comes out and figure this out."

As light worked its way into the cave, the outside world still swirled with blinding white curtains of snow, Puffy flakes in the shifting winds were uncertain on which side of anything they should settle. Wolf rose, went outside briefly, and returned, shaking himself free of the wet chill. He disappeared for a moment indicating there was more depth to his upper ledge than I originally thought. On his return, he again began his watch over me. He was patient, and I'm sure he had a plan. Watching, I began to learn from him. He was studying me as well.

In late afternoon as the wind began to calm, and the snowfall decreased, so did the temperature. The warm draft from the rear of the cave was less effective and I began to shiver even while wearing my warmest wraps. I needed more of a shelter, even in the cave. With the shovel I had salvaged from the wagon, I scooped a berm around my little corner in the cave. The sandy berm would deflect the invading breeze. I made it just perfect to lay in and pile anything insulating over me. The first thing that came to mind was a buffalo robe. But hunters had killed the last buffalo in the area several years ago. I would have to concentrate on skinning a couple of deer. But again, I would have to wait until the bitter cold had less chance of freezing my exposed skin. And I would surely get wet tramping in the snow. I would need a method of drying out my pants and boots.

As I worked through my survival problems, and built my little in cave refuge I realized Pa had taught me a few things. He was sort of like Wolf. He silently did things, let me watch and expected me to figure things out for myself. Back in Coulson, when we were packing up to head back home, I questioned why the railroad clerk was so unfriendly and unwilling to help. I knew Pa was in despair but I questioned why we were returning home with no solutions. Pa gave me an answer that I didn't then, and don't now really understand. But when Pa answered, I learned years ago, not to question again.

He said, "Intelligence is not parceled out equally at birth. You have to use your own to help out those who come up short. As you watch what I've done, then do what I do, but I expect you to skip over the errors and benefit from the good."

Ma taught me differently. Everything was organized into specific lessons. Her classroom had to be crafted from our surroundings, nature, and her initiative. The fire that destroyed much of her and Pa's life left them destitute of all but their personalities. She saved only what was most precious to her. A Bible, a few St. Louis newspapers with pictures and advertisements from her store which were instrumental in my education, a few of her youthful photographs, a sewing-mending kit, and curiously an old English language dictionary. Nature taught me arithmetic when I was put through mental exercises that, for example, required me to count the number of geese in a flock, then divide them so that an equal number will arrive in four different places after three abandoned the trip. But the dictionary had at one time even been used as a punishment.

It was after one of Ma's trips with Pa to Roundup, and I had spent three days with Julie at the Carlson ranch. Julie and I had watched the ranch hands break a wild horse into a saddle bronc. It was a spirited event during which the ranch hands used language I did not understand, the most frequent of which was the use of the word bastard. It seemed quite useful in describing something difficult, mean or unpleasant and was most often directed at the horse. It came in terms of, "Ha, you fell off the bastard. Well, let's see you ride the bastard. No, you get back on the bastard. I ain't gonna let the bastard get the best of me."

A quick learner, I thought I had learned a new word to describe a similar situation. However, back at home several days later, as I was playing horse, straddling one of the corral poles, I lost my grip. I fell, skinning my arm and bruising my forehead on the way to the ground. As any young child would do, I ran to Ma whining for a loving get well hug. When she asked why I was crying, I explained that I was pretend riding one of the corral poles and "fell off the bastard."

Ma switched me with a willow and admonished me to never use that bad word again. Confused, I asked what made a bad word bad. She didn't answer immediately, apparently giving it some thought. Eventually she brought out the tattered old dictionary, and stated, "There are thousands of good words on the pages of this fine book that you may use to describe any situation. Henceforth you will extract ten new words per day from this book and memorize the meaning of each. You will do so until you have memorized not less than one hundred pages." By the time I had completed one hundred pages, I was addicted to using words even Ma questioned, but for which I was never switched.

Seven years have passed; that old book is abandoned on a rotting shelf up in the Musselshell basin, and I still don't know exactly what bastard means. Ma saw that I was equipped with words for every decent occasion, while Pa appeared to be only vaguely aware that I was in the house.

Pa taught me about fires. While Ma saved her precious few things, Pa saved only the horses and a few ranching tools. Indeed, Pa was forgiving, but held out a supreme hate for the flames that robbed him and Ma of their dreams.

Thus, Pa spoke carefully about fire. He taught that smoke was as important, or as destructive as fire. From his lessons I learned to build a fire to warm, cook, dry, or secure myself in the wilderness. I dwelt on his concern about smoke. As I looked across the cave to Wolf, I suspected he would have a similar smoke aversion.

Finally, sitting in my little cave sandbox, I ceased shivering. Just thinking about fire may have helped. My thoughts were:

"There's plenty of dead trees on this hillside; good pine wood that will burn hot. But starting a fire in the cave could be a disaster and smoke both me and Wolf out into the cold. I need to first build a fire outside, and bring a smoking log in to see where the smoke rises, and how fast it escapes. OK, I have matches in my cache, as soon as Wolf leaves, I'll get started."

But again, daylight was fading. Wolf, probably tired of watching me chew dried antelope, trotted out into the fading light. I wrapped up and walked out into the biting cold air. The snow crunched loudly around my boots flipping above the tops as I shuffled sideways across the boulder strewn hill. It would have been easier to keep the snow out of my boots if my pant legs were longer. I knew I was growing, but the bottoms of the pants barely covered the boot tops. No wonder Pa's clothing was beginning to fit. Above, Bull Pine branches sagged under the weight of at least twenty inches of fresh snow. The only disturbances in the blanched terrain were the tracks of Wolf. He had marked his territory, and apparently made his way lower on the hill to where a trickle of water emerged from a pebbled depression. I thought it curious that with the sound of water dripping in the cave, Wolf never made a track in that direction. Perhaps he had a reason – knew something I didn't. Pa's words came to me, "Watch and learn."

The cold made it impossible to work with exposed hands, but I located several nearby dead branches that would serve as firewood. Tomorrow would be a new day of learning. As I worked my way back to the cave, I could see the start of the night sky. Stars are never so bright as they are on a cold winter night. As each new one appeared, it reminded me where I was, and pierced my soul with a new kind of loneliness. I was so small, so insignificant so alone, and so insecure. I returned to the cave. Not even Wolf was there to console me.

It was early in the evening, but I had nothing more to do. The moon and starlight from outside sent a soft glow into the cave. I lay there not moving, to preserve my body heat captured under my thin covering. I heard a faint shuffling sound and looked over to see Wolf entering the cave. But wait! There was more shuffling, and then I realized what I had heard the night before. Wolf was not alone. Lady Wolf had been hiding further behind him out of my sight. She had avoided my detection and apparently only had gone out during the night. I felt better for Wolf, but not safer.

CHAPTER 7   THE HUNT

In spite of the cold I slept well. Perhaps I was getting used to it. I awoke to find Wolf gone, and I assumed his companion also had joined him for a hunt. It was too cold to melt water naturally in the cave, making the exploration of a fire more urgent. I wrapped my hands in a torn piece of canvas that I had used to transport my cache and proceeded to gather wood. After clearing the snow from between three large boulders, I made a base of pine needles and stacked dry wood on top. A fire easily sprang to life with only two matches. I piled on wood until I had to retreat a few steps back to avoid the heat. I filled both buckets with snow which quickly changed to drinking water. After several medium sized sticks had burned to smoking embers, I took a pair of them in hand and entered the cave. To my surprise, the smoke did not curl out the front opening. Nor did it retreat to the back, or even accumulate near the top of the cavern. Small ribbons of smoke rose and slid to the left side near where I had been camping, but spread out along the wall and disappeared into a crack in the roof. I moved the sticks around, being careful not to molest Wolf's domain and the exit path stayed consistent. No wonder I felt a draft in my "bedroom". Warmer air was rising from within the mountain, passing along the wall next to me, and out the roof above. I was quite pleased with the results, but during the time I had been conducting the experiment, a mild breeze had begun stirring the outside air, causing a change in the draft around the entrance. The change caused the smoke to spread wider across the ceiling before exiting through the roof. I knew that Wolf would not enter a cave containing smoke. But I would bet he and Lady would tolerate a bed of glowing coals in the sand on my side of the hotel.

That afternoon I had my first hot meal in days. On a bed of coals, brought in with the shovel, I created hot water. Then I soaked everything I had been eating dry, in the warm solution, and had a soup of meat, apples, berries, and a pine needle tea. Just the warmth of it all was wonderful, and brought my spirits up to new levels. Afterwards I cut branches and constructed racks for drying my clothes and potentially cooking game I planned to harvest.

Near dusk, Wolf and Lady boldly entered the cave, but stopped short when they noticed the changes and most likely caught the smell of smoke. I had hoped that the smoke outdoors would condition them to accepting a small amount of it penetrating into the cave. I received a distrustful look from Wolf. After staring at each other for two days, without thinking, I spoke to him in a soft voice.

"Well hello old friend. Where have you been? I hope you don't mind the decorations. I'll make it up to you as soon as I can get out to go hunting."

Lady immediately scampered to her sanctuary in the back of the ledge, while Wolf walked in a half crouch to his throne of observation. His gaze gave me neither approval, nor rejection.

He watched as if to question, "Why is this necessary."

Two more days passed before I felt it was safe to venture away from the cave to hunt. The snow was still deep, but the cold not as severe. I wrapped the top of my boots with the remaining canvas and took Pa's rifle for a short walk. Tracking was easy in the snow. In a short time and close to the cave, I had taken two large rabbits and two smaller ones. I could have shot more but I didn't want anything to go to waste. At the most I only needed three, but I took an extra one in hopes of making better friends with Wolf.

I skinned and cleaned them outside, away from the cave, keeping the skins in hopes of fashioning some sort of gloves with them. I cut up one hare to eat, put two on the upper storage pole and cut one in half with the intent of enticing Wolf to accept an offering. A fire, a bed of coals shoveled into my sand pit, and I again had a king's meal of fresh meat.

Again, near dusk, Wolf and his partner came into their den to rest before going back out for their night hunt. They had become comfortable with my presence. Even my cautious slow conversation failed to disturb them, and to the contrary often calmed their anxiety.

This evening it was obvious Wolf smelled the activity that had taken place in my kitchen. He continued to sniff the air, probably sensing the fresh meat, over the pungent smell of the pine coals. Capturing his complete attention, I slowly moved from my restricted corner of the cave toward the center and his ledge. In my hand, I held in front of me half of the smaller rabbit. His muscles tensed, but he did not move. I very slowly inched closer, murmuring that everything was OK. With only fifteen feet between us, he raised his upper lip, showed long white fangs and growled. I feared he would pounce any second. I slowly placed the raw meat below him, and back away in a slow crawl, never taking my eyes off of his. He took several moments to make his decision. His eyes flickered between me, and the meat, until he slowly rose into a low crouch as if to pounce on the meat. Instead he maintained his crouched posture and crept up on the meat. He did not touch the morsel until he had sniffed its entire circumference, saw that I had returned to my corner, and licked it for taste. Suddenly he grabbed the offering as if it were a running rat, snatched it into his mouth and jumped back upon his perch.

I waited until he devoured the entire half of the rabbit, bones included and repeated the entire exercise again with the other half. Wolf learned quickly. The second time involved no growling; however, I did not advance any further than my initial approach. He watched just as nervously but correctly anticipated the outcome. I placed the food on the sandy floor and he confidently but slowly retrieved it. Unexpectedly, on his return to his perch, his partner was waiting, to perform her own quick snatch and run. She retreated to her lair, and I could hear her crunching the nights offering.

The next morning was cold, but bright and clear. Pa used to describe cabin fever, and I was getting the equivalent in cave fever. Lady and Wolf spent little time inside, and only to rest or when the weather was absolutely unbearable. My lack of good winter clothing kept me within a short distance of the natural shelter. Because of my limitations I had not seen any of the terrain to the west of the cave. I had only ventured a few yards to gather wood, fearing I would lose my way in the blinding wind and weather. Today appeared to be a good time to explore the hillside to the west.

I fastened my pant tops around my boots, cradled the rifle in my arm and traversed up the ridge to the west. Last evening's breeze had dusted off the pine trees and I was able to stay dry from the knees up. When I reached the top of the hill, the view was amazing. The sun was so bright on the new snow, I pulled Pa's hat low over my forehead and squinted until my eye lids left only tiny slits through which to see.

I thought, "Wolf, if all could see this, your home, you would be the envy of the world." The contrast between the bright snow and the cloudless sky produced the darkest, clearest blue I had ever seen. The undulating hills below, strewn with rough boulders falsely appeared smooth and gentle. Dark green pine trees, hundreds individually shaped, clung to the rough slopes and sprung up between crevasses in the sandstone. From where I stood, on top of the hill, I could see in all directions. Nothing blocked my view for approximately two miles. It was a wonderful place, but the breeze at the top was very chilling.

I could see a few tracks in the snow. Some appeared to be from deer, the others were probably left by Wolf. I decided it was too cold to hunt, and I still had two or three days of meat left in the cave. I set out to return, but foolishly chose a shorter, but steeper route. Within sight of my destination, I stepped on what I judged to be a flat boulder. Instead it was a flat snow drift between two boulders. I fell hard. My foot and leg wedged between the two boulders pinning me tightly clear up to my hip. The rifle fell in the snow beside me, just slightly out of reach.

A rush of pain shocked me so hard it seemed to have no definition. I could not tell if it was coming from my foot, ankle, shinbone, or all three places. The cold snow added to the nerve transmitting confusion and I waited a short time before I began trying to free myself from the stone trap. Thankfully, the boots were too large for my feet and the loose fit allowed me to pull my foot upward out of the boot. My bare shin was severely skinned. The ankle moved, but with considerable pain.

My first thoughts were that if I broke my leg, I would probably have to shoot myself as they do horses, rather than die a slow agonizing death. I wondered if I should crawl to the cave before the shooting so that I would be of some benefit to Wolf, or if I should shoot myself outside here on the hillside, to be shared by all the varmints. In short order I realized this was panic thinking and in the worst of cases I could fashion a splint and heal good enough to walk in two months. "Oh my God, two months? Who would feed me? How could I walk 30 or 40 miles even in two months? No, this leg just can't be broken." Again, I settled myself down just the way I did when Pa died, with a few deep breaths and the cold realization that I must think for myself, slowly and reasonably. But there is no comparison to how alone you can feel when you are looking at your own blood, and there is no one nearby who cares.

I examined the leg. It was missing some skin, and bleeding but everything moved and worked as it should. I could stand on it with no more pain than if I was sitting with it exposed to the snow. I retrieved the rifle from the cushioning snow drift and pried the boot from where it was clamped between the two boulders. I dumped the snow out of the boot, slipped my foot into it and slowly limped toward the cave. As I crawled through the opening I thought with bitter humor, "Well, I won't have any trouble putting together an ice pack."

The foot and ankle throbbed for two days. A large red and purple bulge swelled up on the side of my shin. After five days the ankle was approaching normal, but the lump on the side of my shin was enormous and I could see it was filled with blood, much the same as a blister on the hand fills with clear fluid. I had seen Pa doctor a horse with a similar lump. Pa took his knife and made a cut through the lump to drain the fluid. The lump subsided, the cut healed and the horse was fine. I decided I should do the same.

I took my skinning knife and sharpened it to a fine edge on a sandstone rock. I lay the knife in the bed of coals from the fire until I was sure it was clean.

I held ice and snow on the lump until the skin was numb. Carefully, I let the sharp blade slide up my shin the width of three fingers opening the blood-filled lump. With a little pressure a jelled mass was massaged from the cut and I could immediately feel relief from the constant throbbing. I tied several strands of leather raw hide around the wound to hold it shut until it dried. I washed it regularly with salt water, kept it clean, and expected to be walking very soon. I had to. I was out of food.

Days were passing as I was puzzling how to safely get to Coulson. I reasoned the passage was too far and too dangerous to attempt in bad winter weather. Although some days were milder, Montana territory could develop a storm withing just a few hours. I had not even ventured back to the wagon wreckage to retrieve what remained of the meager supplies. I made that my next project, and thought to combine the trip with a big game hunt. I was tiring of the small birds and animals.

I began at sunrise on a clear morning, carrying only a rope, knife and my rifle. The snow was difficult to traverse, but had blown and melted to half its former depth. I broke a trail through the snow, detouring around a few large drifts, and being careful not to reinjure my still very tender leg. The terrain looked different in its heavy white disguise. I passed by the wrecked wagon, missing it by over a hundred yards and had to backtrack to find it partially buried in snow. I found the remains of the wagon as I had left it, but varmints and rodents had helped themselves to most things edible. A little salt, sugar, barley and corn were still in their sacks, but the flour, and most of the beans were gone. A few seed potatoes remained so I tied them all into a burlap sack.

I built the same kind of sled with broken wagon boards, tied on what I had salvaged, and prepared for my return trek. I planned to return nearer to the cave before I shot anything large like a deer or an elk. I thought if I shared the meat with Wolf and his partner, I should be able to preserve my portion for several weeks, especially in the cold weather. I began tramping my way back toward the cave, dragging the sled behind me, anticipating a much larger load before journey's end. My leg began to remind me that it had not yet fully healed.

The small spring below and to the left of the cave, was evidently a watering hole for wildlife. Deep trails revealing large hoof prints led to and from the source. I searched the hillside looking for a place of concealment with access to the spring. Above me I saw movement that transformed into a small herd of elk. Several large bulls stood proudly in the open with their antlered heads held high. The sunlight was harshly in my eyes, but I could clearly see their outline. I was not hunting for a trophy bull. A smaller tender yearling would better suit my needs. I knelt behind a boulder and aimed, but other boulders were then in my line of sight. I stood again watching for something smaller. Another target appeared. I took a quick shot at the neck; the only part visible of an animal standing next to a large pine tree. It fell. The other beasts fled and I ran up the hill.

Standing by the dead animal, I stared in wonderment. The color was slightly lighter than most elk. There was no dark fur around the neck. It was fat and wide. The horns were straight. I had just shot a branded range cow. Her brown winter coat in the sunlight, did not distinguish her from the elk herd. I could not tell the difference, especially with her standing behind a bull pine tree. During several days of travel, I had never seen a ranch animal. This must have been a stray that wandered for miles and by chance was with the elk.

"Well", I thought, "It's dead now. There's no use in letting it go to waste. Either the wolves, coyotes and lions will eat it, or I will. Anyway, if it was out here much longer, it would get killed by something else. As fast as the elk move, the cow could not possibly keep up. It would soon be singled out by predators." I rationalized that someday I would find the owner and pay him for the animal, but spent little time lamenting over a task so far into the future.

I skinned and cleaned it, just as Pa had shown me. The winter hide was thick and heavy, and just what I needed for warmth in the cave. I rolled the innards out of the way, and cut off the best chunks of meat. A whole cow was more than I could eat even if I stayed here until summer. The challenge would be to keep it from spoiling. It would stay frozen for a few weeks if left outside, or perhaps in the coldest part of the cave. I could dry some, cook some, and wait. . .I had seen Wolf bury what he and Lady could not eat. The sand preserved their cache for several days until they unearthed it during winter storms. Using all the different techniques I should be able to make good use of most of the best meat. The rest of the carcass I would leave above the spring for Wolf and his associates.

I made several trips pulling the sled loads of fresh meat to the cave. Not far from the opening I constructed a "meat bank." Several large rocks, rolled into place created a stone "ice box" where I placed the meat on a bed of sticks and locked the ice box with another boulder that only a huge grizzly could move. The meat would freeze and be safe for several weeks. I busied myself until after nightfall preparing the meat for preservation and keeping it out of the jaws of Wolf and Lady. Throughout it all, they did not appear. Perhaps they had discovered what I had left behind. My last effort before collapsing into sleep was to stretch out the hide to dry. I placed it on a boulder, further into the cave in the draft of warm air. Tomorrow I would place it out in the sun. I retired exhausted and with a mildly throbbing leg.

The next three days passed quickly. I was occupied with smoking, salting and preserving meat, sorting and repackaging the wagon food and working at drying the cowhide. I frequently flexed it over the sunlit boulders to make it pliable. It was going to be my version of a buffalo robe. Meanwhile the leg was feeling much better.

Time and close proximity had tempered Wolf's attitude. He, not Lady, and I had become cautious friends. Wolf allowed me to approach close enough to his platform to feed him directly from my hand. He had not allowed me to touch him, but I had never really tried. He would occasionally lick my salty hand but it was my goal to someday pet him on the head, though his gleaming fangs were a barrier to familiarity.

I think he viewed me with great curiosity. It was good that there was ample food outside of his cave. He never attempted to approach my elevated cache held up on poles, or to steal even a morsel when I wasn't looking. Instead he watched me for hours. Perhaps he thought of me as a child playing with my food. His method of consumption was to snatch it and gulp it down in huge lumps. Chewing seemed to be a time-consuming risk ultimately resulting in less food consumed per second.

I would have enjoyed training him to come to me for food, but that would rob him of his independence and slowly destroy him. I did not wish to tame him. I thought it better that I would become wild myself. Neither of us were going to allow the growth of trust to be ruined by a selfish need to dominate.

CHAPTER 8   DISCOVERY

Clouds had filled the afternoon sky. Another winter storm was threatening to pin Wolf, Lady and me into our palace for an unknown duration. This time we were prepared with food, warmth and water. The only constant sounds were the wind and the oscillating branches of the pines. Wolf was dozing on his ledge above the cave opening and I had fallen asleep on the edge of my sand bed. With all of my senses working together I heard, smelled and saw something; a shadow fell across me. I opened my eyes to see human boots. Near my head, sturdy legs towered upward to form a man. Crow footed eyes suspended above a stringy dark beard glared down at me. With an intense painful feeling of repugnance and fear, I recognized this man; "Mean Morgan."

His first words were, "Well you little bastard, what are you doing here?"

There was that word, and I knew what followed was not going to end well. I was too startled to speak and only stammered, "Why?"

"Cause I just found you where you ain't supposed to be; that's why." He stepped closer to me, his wide belly casting a shadow over my thumping chest.

"How'd you find me?", I asked.

"I been round'n up winter strays for the 'Circle X'. Some ah the herd come clear down here toward the Yellerstone. And I come across a busted wagon – where's your Pa? – and I fallerd yer tracks up to one of what might 'a been one of my cows. And it weren't too hard to faller you and the cow into this stinking cave. Now I suppose yer gonna tell me that there hide with the circle X on it just jumped offen the cow and run in here to make you happy. The wagon kilt your Pa didn't it. So being that cow is dead, and the hide is under your ass, and the meat is in your pot, you is a rustler."

"I didn't kill it on purpose."

"Every rustler that gets catched says that, and you ain't no differ'nt. There ain't many of them good strong cows die of heart attacks. Now 'cause I'm working for Boss Clyde of the Circle X, and 'cause Clyde is a friend of the Sheriff, they both agree that rustlers should be hanged right next to the dead cows they stolt. I figure that's a lot easier'n dragging you back to Roundup with a rope 'cause you ain't got no horse and you'd never make it anyway. So, after I swing you from a tree, I'll take yer scalp to Boss Clyde and git paid a little extre."

He bent down as if to grab my leg and pull me from my corner. I saw it. I saw it right then and not more than an arm's length away, right next to me, and in insane fury I immediately knew the answer. Partially hidden by his coat, but around his neck in plain view when he bent over was a scarf. The only scarf in the world like that belonged to Julie.

"You bastard! What did you do with her?"

He paused, looking confused and then pulled at the scarf grinning. "I sold her. Her Pa owed me money, didn't pay. I found her up at the fossil beds, told her that the Injuns kilt all of 'um at the ranch so I'd take her to safety. So, I took her to Coulson and sold her. Only got a hunnert dollars for her 'cause the dealer said she was too young and undeveloped. Said he'd have to send her to Miles City."

Something new burned within me. Ma's Bible teaching suddenly meant nothing. I hated this man, and it was clear that he didn't qualify for forgiveness. My mind was thrashing in my skull, but was understanding that this hulk probably killed Julie and just said he was going to hang me. My rifle was loaded and, in a panic, I reached for it. What was I thinking? Morgan was already holding his, directing the gun butt to first knock my arm to the ground, followed by a sharp blow to my stomach. I screamed in pain and fell forward. Rolling to the side to avoid another blow, I saw Wolf, who had gone unnoticed, become a dark bounding blur, land on Morgan's back. He yelled as Wolf bit into his shoulder and proceeded ripping down his back and into his thighs. He tumbled Morgan toward my fire pit where he fell face down next to the stone circle. Morgan was trying to get his rifle around to shoot Wolf but couldn't throw off the quick muscular beast nearly his size and weight. Wolf had his teeth into Morgan's buttocks and was jerking his head side to side, bouncing Morgan's entire body, ripping flesh in the process. Only Morgan's heavy clothing kept him from being chunks of raw meat. Morgan tried to roll onto his back, but whenever he exposed his chest, Wolf attacked toward his throat. Morgan tried pushing Wolf to the side but couldn't keep Wolf away from his neck. They were both moving so fast and violently, I couldn't get close enough to help Wolf who was doing fine on his own. Finally, Morgan rolled to his side and got both hands on his rifle. Knowing Morgan would soon make good with the rifle, I picked up one of the largest firepit stones and raised it above my head as Morgan extended one arm, about to shoot. I brought the big rock down full force. It hit him in the upper part of his forehead. He quit struggling immediately.

At first, I didn't realize what I had done. Morgan didn't move. Blood poured from his head, and I could see white bone over his eyes just under a large hole in his forehead. I had used a bolder the size of Morgan's head to smash the life out of him.

Wolf continued his attack, determined to tear the big man into several pieces. He was in such a frenzy; I was afraid to touch him or even get close. I steadily spoke to him in low tones and rose to my feet. When he realized neither Morgan nor I was struggling, he stopped ripping on Morgan and stood next to me, a low growl still coming from deep in his throat. He was intent on dismembering Morgan right there by the fire pit, an act that even my hate wouldn't condone. For the first time, I reached for him. He was extremely agitated and for a moment I thought he might turn on me in a wild defensive lunge. He stepped back, but stopped and looked at me, as if I were a stranger. I slowly held out my hand. He held his position, growling. I rubbed his head. We looked at each other for a few seconds. It was a wonderful once in a lifetime moment. His language I could not understand, but his thoughts I could read with ease. Our bond was now evident. He took a step toward Morgan and I gently held my hand on his chest softly saying, "No." He turned and without looking at me again, trotted back to his perch.

Now I had another body to dispose of. I carefully removed Julie's scarf from the Bastard. It was soiled, but it was still Julie's; light blue with tiny dark blue dots in rows. I put it next to my bed, and drug Morgan out into the deteriorating weather. I would have enjoyed tossing him down the hill to bounce over the moraine of boulders. That would provide little satisfaction if he were discovered. Normal burying on a frozen rock covered hillside was out of the question. I remembered a rabbit run nearly two hundred yards around the next bluff in a deep coulee. Each side of the coulee was rimmed by high loose boulders. It would be easy to cause a rock slide there.

I slid the heavy Bastard through the snow without remorse. I pulled him into the coulee and placed him there at the bottom, face down as if he had stumbled or been knocked over by a rock. I realized I should have put his rifle with him, but I needed both hands free to drag him by his tattered coat. The jagged hole in his blood-soaked buttocks was sickly humorous as I found myself quite proud of the way in which Wolf flew from his perch to nearly cut the hams off of this pig. After climbing to the top of the coulee, I pushed on a huge boulder that was balanced like an egg on a knife. The sandstone base cracked and the big boulder tumbled, breaking thirty feet of the hillside loose, burying the Bastard Mean Morgan under tons of rock.

I felt no guilt, but my mind continued to work defensively. "Morgan had to be a long way from this ranch he was calling Circle X. For sure he didn't walk to get here. There must be a horse. A horse means there is more work to do. If he is missed, and they find the horse, they will find me. How easy it must have been for Morgan to find me. I left tracks as big as a railroad everywhere I pulled my sled. How did I expect not to be found? But then, I really wasn't hiding, was I?"

I located the horse, near the carcass of the butchered cow, along with three more live cows picketed among the pine trees. I turned the cows loose, and chased them to the winds. I rolled up the roped use to contain the cows and carried it with me as I continued pondering my dilemma. I wanted nothing to do with anything belonging to Morgan or Circle X, but began to think more logically about the horse. With a horse, I could ride to Coulson in two or three days. I could turn the horse loose just before I arrived and no one could connect me with it.

"But this is still winter. Do I dare risk three days travel in bad weather? If I don't go now, how do I keep a horse safe out here without anything to protect it from everything that wants to dine on fresh horse meat? There's nowhere I can put him to keep him safe. He needs water and food, none of which I can provide up here on this rocky slope. I will have to go soon."

Night was approaching and I led the horse back near the mouth of the cave, and within the marked territory of Wolf. With the saddle removed and on a long rope, he could defend himself to some extent. I hoped to hear him struggle if he was attacked. Tonight, I would feed Wolf and Lady beef to stay their appetite for horse meat.

The day had ended when I had things settled to where I could contemplate the events of the past few hours. One day ago, I was almost content with being isolated with two wolves in the wilderness blessed with shelter, ample food, water and occupied with my own survival. Tonight, I retire with a new identity. I have suddenly become a cattle rustler, murderer and if I am not careful, a horse thief.

"But I am not any of those. I would never have shot that cow if I would have seen it clearly without the sun in my eyes. Someday I will pay the owner back for his loss. But maybe not, now that Mean Morgan has become the person with all the information. What do I do about him? The only people that know where Morgan is, and what happened to him is Wolf and me. Wolf is not a person and he won't tell anyone. If I would have left Wolf to his own task, he may have killed Morgan. A couple more quick moves and Wolf would have had Morgan's throat. No, I will never mention Morgan to anyone."

I put my hand down and touched Julie's scarf. I put the scarf to my face and nearly retched. All presence of Julie was gone. Only the memory of her image wearing the decorative garment remained.

"How do I know Morgan was telling the truth about Julie. It seems like a tall tale, and I don't really understand it. Why did Morgan keep her scarf to wear as a neckerchief? Was he so angry with Julie's Pa that he punished them all with her abduction? What did he mean when he said he sold her? Who buys people or young girls?"

I remember Ma telling me about a terrible war that happened around New Orleans when she was young because white people were selling black people for slaves.

"But that happened years ago. And Julie is white. Who would buy her for a slave when there are so many strong men looking for work? What did he mean about only getting a hundred dollars because she was not developed? It all sounds like a lie to me, but I have to go to Coulson to find out. The other place Morgan mentioned was Miles City. I think that is further east, but still in Montana Territory. She may still be alive, and I have to go as soon as possible."

As I lay there thinking, I became fully aware how important the horse near the cave entrance was. He was as important as the weather, but each presented their own chances for fatality.

"If I wait for spring weather, that could mean at least a four-week delay. I cannot keep this horse alive here for another month. He has to eat. The dried prairie grass is a quarter mile below the bluff I am living in. The grass is there, but he will have to dig and scrape in the snow for it. If I stake him out down there, he will be vulnerable to wolves, cougars, bears, coyotes and flying vultures. He won't last two nights. If I turn him loose to graze on his own, he'll be gone and I will for sure have to wait until spring to walk the twenty to forty miles. If I leave here tomorrow, I will take the chance of dying among the sage without even a pile of rocks to cover me. I don't even know how far, or how many days I will have to travel. But for me to die, there will have to be a bad storm. We have only had two storms in the several days since Pa died. I now have wraps and hides to protect me from the cold. What good am I if I stay here in the warmth, gorging on 'stolen' beef, talking with a sly non-conversational wolf? The latest storm turned out to be only a mild squall that quickly passed leaving less than an inch of new snow. I believe I can do this."

I began making a mental list of preparations for an early morning departure. I wanted nothing to do with anything of Morgan's. Not his food, his canteen or even his bed roll. Even if he was dead, I felt I would be stealing it from him. My hate was so strong I wanted nothing in sight that was ever associated with him. I realized that I should have buried it all with him in the rockslide. But it was too late for that.

For the first time, I explored the far end of the cave, in the very dim light. I decided it would be wise to also bury anything that could be identified with me. The sand was soft and with a few scoops, the shovel buried what was left my own and Morgan's property in separate locations. I thought that someday if I ever needed to confirm that Morgan had a rifle and threatened me as well as Wolfe, I should preserve it. I was not about to take it with me, so I wrapped it and all of his ammunition in a piece of canvas from the wagon, and buried it in the sand at the back of the cave. There I saw the dripping water; acrid, crusty alkali. No wonder Wolf avoided it.

Upon returning I gazed at one last item. Julie's scarf. I could not take it with me. I had become accustomed to allowing my mind counsel my inner emotions.

"How can I explain it? If she is not alive, how can I convince authorities that I had nothing to do with her demise? I cannot tolerate the thought of burying the scarf near anything of Morgan's. It is evidence that Morgan took Julie. But to what value? He is already dead. Who will punish him more? But I should not totally destroy the scarf. Who knows what strange event may require me to produce it? I must store it where only I will know it exists." And so I did.

CHAPTER 9   ON THE MOVE

I saddled the horse, a strong looking gelding, obviously capable of carrying big Mean Morgan through this rough country. He was a handsome roan, with white socks and one round white spot behind his left ear. During the process I noticed he was branded with a mark I had never seen before, and very "head shy" as if he had been beaten and whipped in the past. It was not surprising considering the temperament of his last owner. I would have to gain his trust in the hours to come. I was going to be small in the large saddle, but that allowed me to tie on several survival items.

The cowhide was essential to survive an unexpected blizzard, and the old blanket also kept me off the ground. Of course, Pa's rifle rode in the scabbard to which I also attached the worn old shovel. A length of rope lay coiled around the saddle horn. I wrapped my feet with rabbit skins and slipped them into my oversized boots, keeping additional skins for gloves. Meat, dried, salted, and fresh was packed along with matches. One small pan, saved from the wrecked wagon was stowed with Pa's old canteen. I cut four lengths of leather to wrap around the horse's legs covering the canon from the fetlock to the knee. Pa showed me how to do this to prevent the crusted snow from cutting the legs of a horse as a result of hours of tramping through drifts. Hopefully, there would be little use for them.

It was still early morning and I was ready to go. I had a nervous anxious stomach and a saddened heart. I knew whatever was ahead would surely be less secure than "Wolf Cave." I was most saddened by having to leave Wolf. Neither he nor Lady were in the cave when I wakened and had not been seen during my preparations. Perhaps Wolf was angry with the audacity of my putting a live horse near his door. I felt I owed him. He gave me the gift of a continued life. As a departing gift, I set out all of the stored meet I had preserved. He and lady could have a banquet in my memory. As I mounted the horse, I knew I would never see Wolf again. He was a powerful friend during a tumultuous time. Turning the horse to the south, I understood that whatever time is left for me, I shall never encounter a friend so rare.

* * *

At first the snow was deep and crusted, and I contemplated lacing the horse's legs to prevent early lacerations. Not more than a mile from our beginning, I dismounted and laced the protecting leathers around the forelegs of Horse. It was obviously a new experience for him because he resisted the effort and tried to break away. More than once I considered my fate if the horse broke and ran into the distance without me. My hands were red and stiff from the cold when I climbed back into the saddle. Horse kept straining against the reins, making it impossible for me to keep my hands in my pockets. Eventually I calmed him enough to pocket one hand at a time.

But Horse didn't like the leathers and frequently spooked when he saw his own leg reach out before him. After nearly toppling from the saddle, I removed the leggings as soon as we advanced out of the bluffs. Already the snow was not as deep and I could steer Horse around the wind stacked mounds.

We followed the drainage cuts to the south, however they slowly turned to the east. To maintain our southward course, we discontinued following the draws and again returned to some of the timber and rocky bluffs.

Horse willingly kept a good pace and by midday we had traveled several miles when I became concerned with a new problem. Horse needed water but every narrow stream was frozen. He also needed a midday rest where there was reasonable dried prairie grass for food. Finding both in the same area was difficult.

On his own, Horse found an actively running stream with ice thin enough to break with my old worn shovel; the rocks still being covered with snow and frozen to the ground. He drank his fill while I scraped snow from a good stand of grass growing on the southern sunny side of the hill. I let him eat and rest for what felt like an hour while I sat and enjoyed the sun. Horse was beginning to feel more comfortable with me, and he was my line to a new life. I had to take good care of him until we got to wherever that new place was. I remembered my Pa telling me,

"If you're far out, and kill your horse, you might as well shoot yourself next."

We continued south until the sun was beginning to wear its orange departure warning. A small dry creek had been leading us south, but had occasional pools of water under breakable ice caps. Bunch grass was abundant. Horse and I made camp next to a cluster of sage, there being no pines nearby.

I ate little, still bothered by a nervous stomach. I would be much more at ease if I could get to my destination without Horse, but the reality of not even knowing where I was did not provide the confidence to foolishly tramp into the wilderness in rabbit skin socks stuffed into oversized boots. A warm fire under a chunk of beef would have changed my mood, but I was afraid smoke, and the light of a fire might attract the attention of some wayward traveler. Unaccustomed to telling tall tales, or outright lies, I was unprepared to explain my presence, or my possession of Horse. The animal was branded, but I knew nothing of the origin of the mark and my ignorance would be quickly exposed. I had to avoid everything, and everyone until I got to Coulson.

The night was cold, as I expected. Wrapped in two blankets and covered with the cowhide I suffered little. Horse was tethered to the clump of sage, and occasionally circled around me, causing the rope to skitter over the cowhide and my curled-up body. The first time it occurred, I was so startled I was fortunate to not have shot Horse, my foot or anything else out in the dark. Horse rewarded me by pooping near my head rest, causing me to re-arrange the entire bed. Again, it was a learning experience.

The dawn came very slowly; an eerie slowness that forebode change and a new concern. A heavy cloud cover had developed during the night. Dark grey skies composed of low hanging snow clouds were beginning to wrap around the sandstone buttes. What lie ahead was large open areas where wind and snow in a Montana spring mixture could be fatal. I had to decide whether to move on south or to retreat back into the buttes for shelter and wait out the advancing storm.

As I broke camp, I watched the rate the clouds were moving across the rock pillars a mile or more behind me. Their speed told me that a cold wind would soon be cutting through my ragged clothing. Even Horse was nervously pacing in a wider radius around his picket. To head out into open prairie would be foolhardy. I climbed up on horse and headed back up toward the bluffs.

As I proceeded back into the territory from where I had come, the strange battle between mind and soul began.

"You should not return in this direction. You must leave under any and all circumstances, for in these hills and coulees you are a cattle rustler, a horse thief and a murderer. Delay your departure and you will be claimed as such."

While the thought was frightening, reason prevailed over my fears. My intentions had always been good, and I knew I should not allow myself to be claimed by death like so many who had not the will, or as Pa said, the "parceled out intelligence" to survive. I had to backtrack to save myself and my only transportation to a new life. No one knew of my transgressions, and if I remain of sound mind, it shall always be my inner most secret. I rode onward toward the steep sandstone bluffs, now only a mile away.

Shelter from the wind was important, but snow often drifts on the lee side of objects, covering the shelter side in a solid cold crust. As the first flakes began to fly horizontally past me, I attempted to find a place that would save both me and horse. My best discovery was a large pine with a wagon sized boulder fifteen feet to the side.

I tied Horse to the tree, with plenty of rope to allow him to constantly be near the tree and still keep his rump turned into the wind. I scraped a body sized depression next to the boulder and filled it with branches I ripped off of the big pine. With the horse blanket spread over the pine boughs I hoped to be somewhat insulated from the frozen ground. After gathering up several hat sized rocks, I rolled out the cowhide and weighted its edges down with the stones. Rifle, dried food and a small amount of water were placed under the cowhide and the saddle was set near my head.

By now it was snowing as if the winter sky's entire supply of white fluff needed to be dumped upon earth this single morning. It was difficult at first to determine which direction the wind was coming from because the snow was swirling in multidirectional patterns around all objects. Soon a steady howl was created by a blizzard out of the northwest.

I climbed under the cowhide and covered my head to wait. I was surprised by the comfort but concerned by the creeping cold from the edges of my covering. I didn't hear Horse moving. He had his rear to the wind and stayed near the tree for whatever windbreak it provided.

Once again, I had nothing to do but wait in the dark under the cover of my shelter and think. When lying powerless on the ground it was easy to sink into self-doubt.

"I let all of my plans be disrupted by the appearance of Morgan and then his horse. Had it not been for Horse, I would still be cozy, sharing beef with Wolf. I know in my heart that spring won't come to this territory until at least April. But then, I don't even know what day it is now. I can probably survive this blizzard, but if Horse dies, I will surely follow; just in a different place. But what kind of plans were disrupted? Did I really have a solid fool proof plan, or was I still searching for a solution?"

As usual, after a round of self-pity, I began to think positively.

"This storm can't last more than a day or two at the most. Horse can last that long. As soon as the wind dies down just a little, I will get up and check on him. I know that horses and cows can stand immobile in a storm so long that their nostrils freeze over and they suffocate. I can't let that happen to Horse. I'll get up soon and swat him in the face. Darn that horse anyway, he may be my savior or cause my death, but I am doing the thinking for both of us, and what little control I have over this precarious life will get us through.

I lay there most of the day. Near sunset, the wind began to subside. I slid out of my cocoon to check on Horse. He was still standing with his rear to the northwest with his head down. His face was crusted with snow and a large bunch had fallen onto his backside from the tree above him. I reasoned that his thick hair was insulating him from the snow, while the snow was keeping the cold wind from penetrating his winter coat. I brushed his face clear and left the snow on his rump. If he wanted to, he could shake himself clear. It was good to hear the wind had stopped, but the snow was still falling. From the looks of the darkening sky, it would probably snow most of the night.

I awoke probably around midnight, breathing deep, and struggling for air. I felt as though I was suffocating. I was comfortable and warm, but could not seem to get enough air. As I became more conscious of my problem, I realized I had additional weight on my body. It had to be from snow. I had completely covered my head under the cowhide and snow had sealed me under my covering so well that I had consumed most of the oxygen within. I rolled back the hide and felt the quick bite of the cold air. I saw a faint glimmer above me. Two stars were penetrating the thinning cloud cover. The sun was going to come up again tomorrow.

* * * *

The dawn struck me on my left side, riding south. Horse appeared as willing to travel as I was. The long delay from the storm was hard on him, but the snow was light and not as deep away from the bluffs. We traveled hard all day, both of us becoming conditioned to the routine; up one hill, down the other, around a line of bluffs, across a barren basin, sight another butte to the south and travel toward it.

By late afternoon, I noticed that the terrain was generally sloping gently downhill. Then suddenly as if a door had opened, I could see a valley off in the background, then the familiar tops of barren cottonwoods. This had to be the Yellowstone River. There was very little snow down in the valley.

I worked Horse to the edge of a high cliff bordering the river below. I had seen these cliffs before when we traveled up river from Pompey's Pillar to Clermont and then Coulson. There were occasional breaks leading down to the river. I resolved to find one of these breaks and camp next to the river. But how should I know whether to proceed east or west?

I pictured the valley, and Coulson as Pa and I left after our heart wrenching railroad inquiry. Near Coulson, the river again ran next to tall sandstone cliffs, but the cliffs were to the south of the river. Probably the course wobbled across the valley to both sides of the cliffs, but I remembered Coulson was on the north side, down in the valley.

As I was pondering the directional dilemma, I saw what appeared to be the beginnings of railroad construction far out in the valley below.

"OK", I thought, "I'm heading west."

After only a mile I found a gentle sloping gully guiding us five hundred feet below to the water's edge. I made camp there among cottonwood trees and brush. There was no trail nearby and I felt confident no one would discover our presence. As I looked up the steep hillside bordering the river, I saw the sizable opening of a cave. The sight sent a pang of regret and loneliness deep into my senses. I wondered how Wolf was doing. Would he even miss me?

The weather was much better down in the valley. The ice on the river had broken up near our camp and geese were plentiful along the shore. Horse and I spent a quiet night near the river and were well rested by morning.

One more day and I should be there. Horse was finding his way along the north rim of the Yellowstone valley. Occasional breaks and gullies caused several detours and most game trails led down to the river which then became impossible to travel. The river was still flowing with snow and irregular ice chunks. The snow up on the rim was passable and I had given up on lacing up Horse's legs. His few cuts would heal on their own. After all, I was soon going to turn him loose to fend for himself, and some other lucky soul could explain the origin of his brand. Morgan died of his own accord, which no one would ever discover or learn about, and by now I was firmly convinced I was not, nor would ever be a cattle rustler or a horse thief.

Traveling up river, our direction turned south again. I believed I was approaching Coulson. I could see faint signs of smoke hanging beside the cliffs in the distance. I judged that the town might be five to eight miles away. I cautiously rode three more miles and decided I could not risk bringing Horse any closer. It might still be a half-day walk but I was sure I could arrive before dark.

During the last two days of travel, I tried to develop a plan for arriving at Coulson. An eerie similarity between my Pa and me plagued my conscience. I'm aware that I too have embarked on a journey, out of desperation, with no prioritized purpose or definite plan, other than to find a new way to survive. It's strange! Pa is gone, but I am understanding him more in his absence.

Instead of questioning Pa, I began to question myself:

"I must be honest with myself. The most important thing in life for me right now is to find Julie, or determine her fate. But I cannot accomplish that if I cannot survive on my own. The first priority must be to secure some type of shelter and employment. The thought is frightening, bringing back the stomach turmoil, because I have never had a job, and don't really know how to proceed to get one. I've had chores assigned to me by Ma and Pa, but they weren't for the purpose of earning anything. The chores were just to help us get by. I guess the idea of working must be the same, they just give you something for the effort, and you have to give it back to someone else so you can eat and sleep."

As I looked to the southwest, I could see several buildings scattered out in the flat, but close to the river where it wandered next to sandstone cliffs. That had to be Coulson. It was time to step into reality and actually live through this day to which I had given so much thought.

I rode to a small gully holding a crooked pine to its side. I took the saddle from Horse and placed it next to the tree. I could carry the saddle into town and sell it. But then I would be benefitting from Morgan's death, and would feel like a thief. Although I had not a penny in my pants, I wanted nothing to do with anything belonging to Morgan. I roughly cut the cinch of the saddle to make it appear that some bronc may have scraped it off contacting the branches. I buried the bridle further away on the opposite side of the gully. With a sigh and a quiet thank you, I swatted Horse on the rump and made sure he galloped back to the north. Everything of value from the saddle that I could carry was wrapped in the cowhide. The shovel was left behind. After strapping my rifle on top of the pack I ran a loop of rope around it and over my shoulders hoisting it up on my back. It was heavy, but at least I didn't have to lug it uphill in a snowstorm. It was going to be a two-mile hike and when I arrived, I wanted it to look as though I had hiked twenty

East end of Clark's Fork Bottom, looking south. Coulson in the distance.

All photographs – Courtesy Western Heritage Center, Billings, Montana.

Coulson looking east.   McAdow's store and Lump's Laundry in foreground.

Main Street, Coulson, Killen & Co.'s Saloon on corner.

Freighter's outfit on main street, Coulson.   Looking northeast.

CHAPTER 10   COULSON

I trudged into Coulson after walking two hours under my load. Again, I had forgotten to carry water. Fortunately, this time the weather around me was cold, but dry enough to make me question my judgment. Coulson was a strange place. People just looked at me as I met or passed by them. Few spoke other than a brief nod. I didn't realize at the time that my disheveled appearance may have contributed to their silence.

Slowly walking through the mud, and over the wagon ruts I took better notice of the town that I had when first seeing it from the back of the freight wagon. It had grown, even since my last viewing. There was a saw mill near the river, a hotel and restaurant, a saloon, a general store, something that looked like a bakery, and a building advertising it was a laundry. The central road was a frozen mass of ruts running parallel to boardwalks constructed of rough sawn planks. There were also more people moving among the buildings. Most seemed busy, except a group of men were loitering in front of one of the largest buildings which seemed to be a store.

As I passed by one of the saloons, I heard strange sounds from within. What I heard was not coming from human voices, but it was music. Ma had sung short songs and hymns to me, but this had to be coming from something she once described as a piano. I heard real music for the first time. It was wonderful, but I had no time to stop and listen. I resolved to return at my first chance.

When I approached the large building labeled "Headquarters", I stepped up onto the wide board platform at the buildings front and sat down on a bench near the entrance. My intent was to observe and listen; to learn and when appropriate ask some helpful questions.

Several older men were conversing on the other side of the entrance, paying me no notice. I set down my pack, approached them and asked where the nearest place was to get a drink of water. Two looked at me strangely with one of them saying, "There's a pump out back of the store." The other one added, "Young feller, you look like a mule that just broke loose from the pack train."

I smiled and thought, "Great, that's just the image I wanted."

Taking my pack with me, I found a tall iron pump with a cup hanging on a wire next to the handle. I drank and washed my face for the first time in days. Not in a rush to return to the store front, I lingered by the pump, observing the back of several of the buildings bordering the main street. Many were cluttered and littered with abandoned trash. I could not identify several of the discarded items. Some stores thought to put out barrels to contain the trash, but most were overflowing. Pages from old newspapers wadded themselves into niches between tumbleweeds. Several outhouses were indiscreetly located behind various stores, their leaning structures exposing the secrets the collapsing sand beneath them failed to hide. I thought it might be possible to obtain employment cleaning the exterior of the buildings. But then I would need a horse to haul away the refuse. I needed to explore more and also inquire about the railroad. I noticed there was still much activity around the Northern Pacific Office.

While I was musing my next venture a young man, possibly two years my senior emerged from between two buildings and approached the pump. He spoke not a word until he had filled the water cup. Turning, he glanced at me with the first friendly face I had seen in months, chirping, "Hi bub, how ya doin?"

Eager to speak with a real person, I replied as my mother had taught me, "I'm fine, thank you. How are you?"

His mouth opened, but not to drink from the full cup in his hand. His clean white teeth shown through thin lips as he tipped his head to the side and looked me over from wide brimmed hat to short pants barely covering the tops of oversized boots. Pa's coat sleeves hung over the backs of my hands while portions of the makeshift rabbit hide gloves stuck out of the pockets. My pants hadn't been washed since Pa and I left our Musselshell dugout. My roped together pack lay near his feet.

He inquired, "What's your name?"

"Tobias Hawthorn", I said, "They call me Toby."

"Tobias, Huh? Wow! OK Bub, my name's Eddy."

Eddy had a friendly attitude and I needed the help of anyone who would talk with me. He was only a little taller than me, but very muscular. His full head of curly dark brown hair covered the tops of his ears and blended with wide eyebrows. His brown eyes flicked quickly around him picking out detail he seemed to be secretly storing for future use. He had a weathered look about him, except his clothing appeared new. He wore new Levi Strauss pants that I had only seen in Ma's pictures. A new looking shirt fit him well, topped by a coat matching the pants.

Eddy asked, "Where you from?"

"Up North."

"How far?"

"Musselshell Basin."

"Where's your folks?"

"Both died."

"That's too bad. You all by yourself then?"

"Yup."

"Where ya stayin?"

"Don't know, I just got here."

"Where's your horse?"

"Don't have one, I walked."

Eddy paused and looked me over again. He said slowly as if I might not have understood his question, "You're telling me you walked all the way here from the Musselshell in the middle of winter, all the way by yourself; walked with no horse. Your boots don't even look like they made the trip."

My first big lie was about to be formed. Pa always said the truth would serve you better in all circumstances, so I told Eddy about Pa, the wagon, Wolf, and the cave. I left out Mean Morgan, and was vague about the distance of the cave to Coulson, thinking if pressed, I could claim the cave I saw above the bank of the Yellowstone. When I finished I felt like a rat eyed liar.

Eddy seemed impressed, accepted my story for the time being and asked, "How much money ya got, cause anyplace here costs a bunch to stay in."

I confessed, "I don't have any."

Eddy stared at me again and said, "None? What'd you do with it?"

"Nothing! I don't have any. I've never had any. I've never had any use for money. I've never even been to a store before I walked into this town."

Eddy whistled. "OK Bub, OK. I'm staying in a camp at the edge of town. It's a brush shelter, but we got room for one more."

I picked up my pack and followed much relieved. Maybe Eddy was my new Wolf.

Eddy's camp was no isolated hideout. In a gully depression surrounded by cottonwoods, were several other primitive dwellings, from small tepees to stick lean-tos patched together in half circles, their back sides against the northwest wind. A few shelters consisted of only board slabs nailed against the side of cottonwood trees. Branches laced together formed the roofs. Huddled bodies could be seen in various positions within the shelters. A few sat beside smoking rock ringed fires. Eddy's claim consisted of a three-sided lean-to, roofed by a tattered canvas stretched over saplings, and weighted down by additional brush. The ground underneath was covered with dry broom grass. It was big enough to shelter four people and store as many saddles and bed rolls. However, no horse rigging was present.

Eddy pointed to the windy side of the shelter and said, "You can put your stuff over there against the wall. Like everybody else, my friend Jim and I are staying here 'till we can get on with the railroad. They are supposed to start building a bridge across the river between here and the place the railroad is calling Billings. By then it should be spring and livin' should be a little easier. I see you have a good bed roll. You better hide that rifle or some drifter will steal it! What are your plans?"

As Pa would say, Eddy was "quick at prying the lid off the pot." I did not want to tell him everything. Many of Ma's Bible stories taught me to go forth silently listening, however I wanted desperately to gain his confidence and uncover his local information.

Admitting only to myself that my main mission was to learn about Julie, I chose not to mention her until I learned more about this place to which Morgan claimed he brought her. I answered cautiously.

"I need to find a way to support myself. Without money, I can't buy anything, and I'll soon not even have rifle shells to hunt with. I can start a fire, but matches are a lot better if you can afford to buy them. I'm hoping the railroad will give me a job."

Eddy asked, "Well, what can you do? You're tall enough, but you ain't the strongest guy on the river."

"That doesn't matter. I can drive horses. I can load wagons and tie ropes and chains. You don't have to be Paul Bunyan to work on the railroad."

Eddy frowned, "Who's he?"

"Oh, he was a logger back east."

"How'd you know him?"

"He was in stories my Ma used to tell me."

"Well that ain't got nothin' to do with you feeding yourself!"

No, I guess not. But I can read and write, and maybe they need that someplace."

Eddy was quiet for a moment and said, "Well, that's more than anyone around here can do."

As we talked, another tall young person approached. He wore a tattered western hat, perched above stark Indian features. His broad face, black hair, dark eyes and prominent nose presented an attractive appearance. He too looked strong and muscular. I noticed immediately that he was dressed in the same type of clothing as Eddy. Except for the hat and boots, they matched perfectly.

"This is Jim", Eddy said. He's Crow. He sleeps on the far side from you."

Turning toward Jim, he explained, "This is, what'd you say your name was bub? Oh yah, Toby.

Toby ain't got no folks and is even broker than you and me, and I told him he could hang around for a few nights until he figures out what he's made of."

Jim nodded a simple hi sign and sat down in the lean-to.

From the introduction I quickly got the message that I probably was not going to be welcome as a permanent fixture. I was not that concerned. I would just as well prefer to build my own shelter.

The evening was passed with my new friends eating a light meal of dried food. I contributed very little and fasted, not wanting to expose my shrinking store of dried meat I had brought from Wolf cave. I was not selfish, but could not afford to share, when I had no idea what tomorrow would bring. Most of what I ate would turn the stomach of a cast iron dog, but I was accustomed to desperate rationing. We retired early, mostly because of the cold, and fading light. Both of my new friends admired my cowhide cover. I slept much warmer than they.

CHAPTER 11   EMPLOYMENT

The next morning came with a light snow. Jim rose early and returned with a metal can of beans and some coffee. We built a small fire and had coffee, something I had tasted only two or three times in my life. I thought that someday I would have coffee every morning I desired. But today I had to figure out how to earn supper.

Eddy said that the railroad office did not open for business until 8:00 O'clock. Time by the numbers was not something I was used to, and I did not have a watch. Sunup and sundown changed with the seasons, and I knew midmorning, midday, midafternoon, and evening by observing the solar positions. Pa trained me to know about how long an hour was by how long it took for the sun' to cast a shadow that moved between two sticks he placed along an arc.

I wanted to be among the first in line at the office, so I positioned myself near the office door and waited. Several other men came to the office, tried the locked door and complained that "they are late." I patiently waited while others cursed and left.

About midmorning, a middle-aged man, different from the puffy faced clerk I knew from our previous visit, opened the door, and retreated to an inner office. The door to the inner sanctum remained open, but I did not follow him. I politely sat in the chair in front of the desk bearing the sign, "Employment." I dreaded the thought of the cranky old man appearing only to reject my anxious pleas to work, but I was prepared to offer my best argument.

Not long after I sat down, the muffled voices in the inner office became louder. Two men were arguing bitterly; one attempting to command the other to achieve a difficult task. One voice boomed low, the other screeched high.

The higher voice was saying, "How the hell did I know the old man was going to die. He didn't say anything and wasn't sick."

The lower voice growled, "Of course he didn't' tell you he was going to die. He just kept eating so many of those stinking cigars they finally killed him."

High Voice, "What really happened?"

Low Voice, "Yesterday afternoon, the old fool just slumped over his desk and croaked from a heart attack. At least that's what that sawbones over at the hotel said. You should have had a backup clerk. You had to know the old air bag wasn't going to last forever."

High Voice, "Well I don't have a backup, so what do you want me to do?"

Low Voice, "We got a bridge to build and rails to set, and people coming into town to work, so get your ass out there and hire another clerk."

High Voice, "Boss, there ain't one in fifty that can read and write. They sign their names with something that looks more like the brand on a horse's ass than a signature. They can't figure two times two. So don't look for that to happen overnight."

Low Voice, "Unless you find a clerk, you will be working day and overnight, cause I'm not sending word back east that track building is halted because we can't find a simple literate clerk."

A door slammed and a middle-aged man emerged from the rear office. He approached the employment desk and sat in the chair without even looking at me. I took a deep breath and said, "I can read and write."

He jerked his head up off his hands and said, "Yah, I'll bet. Let's hear you spell Minneapolis."

I distinctly spelled, "M-i-n-n-e-a-p-o-l-i-s." Then he said, "How about Minnesota?"

Again, I carefully spelled, "M-i-n-n-e-s-o-t-a."

Then he said, "How about arithmetic?"

I started to spell "A-r-i-t"; and he interrupted me saying,

"No, for God sakes, I mean can you do arithmetic?"

By now I was gaining confidence. I said, "Sure."

He asked, "What's 3 times 42 plus 11?"

At home we didn't have a pencil, or paper to waste, resulting in Ma teaching me to figure in my head. The problem presented was elementary to solve using what Ma called the tens rounding method. I thought 3 times 4 is 12 add a zero because it was 40 not 4, making at total of 120, 3 times 2 is 6 plus 10 more is 16 making the total 136 plus one more is 137. It takes much longer to explain the method than to think it and I gave him the answer within seconds without writing anything down.

"One Hundred Thirty-Seven", I blurted.

The man looked at me, took a pencil and figured it himself. He repeated the exercise with several more problems getting almost instantaneous answers and finally said,

"Well I'll be damned!"

Then he asked, "How old are you?"

I inquired, "What day, or Month is this?"

He said, "March 11, 1882"

I realized it was my birthday and I proudly boasted, "I'm fifteen years old."

He squinted, took off his gold rimmed little round spectacles and rubbed his eyes.

"You're a little young, but don't tell anyone how old you are, and I will hire you to sit behind this desk and take names. You'll have to count and total workers, horses and some machinery. You'll have to write down the names and post them on the wall. You take the name of every person that comes in here, but if it looks like they can't do heavy work, you put a zero by their name in the tablet. We won't post them on the wall. If they have draft horses they can work with, they will get paid extra, depending on the type of team they are driving.

If you got questions, you come to the back office, but think for yourself, because I have my own work to do. I'll pay you a dollar a day. If you do good work for a month, I'll pay you a dollar and half. Your supplies are in the desk. The water pump and the outhouse are back of the building. Keep the back door locked cause we only want them coming in through the front.

He turned, and walked back into his office. He didn't even ask my name. I couldn't help thinking that any moment, he might return and say something like, forget it kid, I changed my mind. But men were coming back into the office and starting to stare at me.

I located a tablet, pencil and straightened the sign. I brushed the cigar flakes from the desktop, scraped away what looked like dried slobber, and motioned for the first in line to come over to my new position. I had closely observed the old puffy faced clerk who had spoken with Pa and knew the script. I took the pencil into my red, rough chapped hand; gripped it with fingers that had not formed a letter in almost a year. My first day of work, ever, had begun.

The tasks were quite simple and I soon became relaxed with the work. At my discretion an additional column was added to the tablet that introduced experience to the applicant's information.

The morning went smoothly, with Mr. High voice checking on my progress only twice. He never bothered to ask my name, thus I thought it precocious to ask his. Each time he looked at the tablet, he murmured words of approval, and returned out of sight to the rear of the office, which I had not yet been invited to view.

My working office measured approximately fifteen feet square and was large enough to accommodate two desks, although it only contained one. The desk faced the door, with windows both to my left and right. Bare wood floors were adorned only with mud from the rutted road out in front of the building. To my judgement, it was a wonderful place to be.

Shortly after noon, Mr. Low Voice appeared and approached me for the first time. He was not as big as he sounded, but very confident in manner. He walked straight up to me and said, "Hey kid, I'm glad you came in. My name is Tom. Tom Teel. I'm chief surveyor for this area of the Northern Pacific."

I rose, and said, "Thank you Sir. I am happy to be here. My name's Tobias and I'm called Toby."

"Toby, well that's a good name. Now Vick, Mr. Pulaski, who also works in the back office, tells me that you write a pretty good sentence. Is that right?"

"Yes Sir, I can write."

"Well surveying is my job, and I never have liked writing letters, maybe because I'm not good at it. But I have to write a very important letter to the main office of the Northern Pacific, maybe even to the office of the President. We've been talking about what we have to say and ask for, but have to be careful how we go about it. Maybe you could write it all down for us."

"Yes Sir, I'll try. What do you want to say?"

"Well, we have a problem with the living conditions out here at the end of the line building the road. We have no place for the workers to sleep, eat, get any supplies, or even get messages back to headquarters about problems or supplies. If people are hungry, wet and freezing at night, it doesn't matter how much we pay them, they work a little bit and are gone. We need to take better care of the work force so they don't get sick, and we can't even doctor the injured."

I thought about some of Ma's lessons and discreetly suggested, "Maybe we should just ask for the most important things and keep the letter simple. It sounds like you need tents, a cooking place and food."

"Yeah, that's it. Good tents we can move. A couple of cooks with a well-equipped cook shack, and some high calorie food. Then they need to devise some sort of message system so we can speed up the supply line. The best thing would be to complete the telegraph line."

Mr. Teel thought quietly at the side of my desk, and said, "OK kid, you write up a few sentences. Vick and I will look them over, polish up the letter, and maybe have you pen it out if you have a good hand with ink. Close up the office for the day and get after the letter."

I tore a new sheet of paper from the tablet and began writing.

March 11, 1882

Honorable Gentlemen in Management,

I pardon your attention to several situational obstacles impeding the advance of track construction to and beyond the Coulson – Billings Yellowstone river crossing.

Our company is striving to recruit and retain men of initiative and ambition who are imperative to our success. However, deplorable conditions within our encampment obfuscate reasonable remuneration and exacerbate corps attrition.

We respectfully suggest minimal articles of comfort be procured to dissuade desertion to include tents and cots for shelter and recuperation, food with high caloric content, complete with a fully staffed cook shack. Lastly, improved communication would markedly increase our rate of supply replacement and production.

These essentials are requested at your earliest convenience to enable the Northern Pacific Railway to boldly advance beyond the Bozeman pass by January 1883.

Respectfully,

Tom Teel

Chief Surveyor

Coulson

When I finished, wanting to see the back offices, I carried the letter to the door from which I heard the earlier conversation and knocked. I heard Mr. Teel answer and walked in. I placed the letter on his cluttered desk. Because he barely gave me notice, I retreated back to my front of the building, and pretended to be busy until I heard him coming my way. I turned to see him looking at the letter, then to me, then back at the letter, walking blindly up to my desk. By his expression, I was quickly concluding he was not pleased with the composition. I waited for him to say something, but it was a long uncomfortable pause while he apparently re-read the entire message. Then he finally spoke.

"Toby, this is great – I think. But I'm not sure I understand part of it. What's this word here, this mastu-no, no, exacter, no –

"Exacerbate", I interrupted, "It means to make worse."

"Oh, OK."

"Where did you learn to write like this?"

"My Ma taught me. She's dead now though. She taught me to read too. We had two books, the Bible and the dictionary. I read the Bible a couple of times, and memorized a lot of the dictionary."

"You memorized the dictionary?"

"Sure, Ma use to make me do it when I was bad, but then when it got to be fun, she quit making me, and I just did it for a while most every day. She used to make me practice writing letters too. I even wrote letters to the President of the United States, but we never mailed them because we didn't have a post office."

"Where'd you come from?"

"Up by the Musselshell Basin."

"Your dad dead too?"

"Yes."

"What did he die from?"

"It's a long story."

"Yes, I suppose so. Sorry"

After pausing a moment, he asked, "How old are you?"

The instructions about concealing my age that Mr. High Voice provided flashed through my mind and I didn't' know how to answer.

I hesitantly replied, "I'm not sure."

Mr. Teel gave me a stern look and said, "What do you mean, you aren't sure?"

I realized that no matter the instructions, it was not going to do me any good to begin my first conversation by lying to the boss.

I explained, "When the other gentleman gave me instructions, he told me not to tell anyone how old I was. I don't know why he said that, but I'd rather say I'm not sure than lie."

Mr. Teel laughed, and said, "That's a great answer kid, but I need to know the truth. How old are you really?"

"I just turned fifteen. Why is it so important?"

"The company doesn't want to hire anyone who isn't at least sixteen. Also, the deputy sheriff around here is a bit of a butt about not having kids hang around getting into trouble. He usually ships kids out that aren't sixteen or over. He's an old trapper turned sheriff. He has a terrible reputation and everyone's afraid of him, so we leave him alone and get along best by doing what he says."

That sent an immediate fear deep into my stomach. I just told this stranger enough to get myself thrown out of town. I looked at him wistfully and said,

"Mr. Teel, it doesn't matter how old I am, I still have to find a way to provide for myself."

He looked at me, eyes glistening, "Toby, I understand. I think we can protect you here. No one knows how old you are, and I surmise you were born at home up in the Territory. It's commendable that you were raised to always tell the truth, however sometimes it is OK to stretch the truth just a little when it is absolutely a good thing to protect yourself. From now on I think you should tell anyone who inquires, you were born on this day, March 11th in 1864. That would make you sixteen today, the day we hired you. I will complete the papers to reflect that information, and it will be our secret. OK with you?"

"Yes Sir, thank you."

"Fine then, *'As the twig is bent, so grows the tree'.*"

"Yes Sir, also a belief of my Ma. I do understand."

As a result of his consultation about truth and necessity, an idea sprung into my mind. "Sir, I have a related question, that I have not shared with anyone."

He was turning toward his office, but stopped and again looked back at me. "And what would that be?"

"I have a twin sister." My Ma died first, but when my Pa died this last fall, some people split us up and were going to take care of us. I left on my own, but my sister was left with people that I didn't trust. I was told they brought her here to Coulson to work. Is that possible? She's not sixteen either? I would really like to find her."

Mr. Teel grimaced and began explaining. "There are very few women in town, and no girls. A couple years ago the law caused many of the working women to leave. Since then a few have returned but operate more discretely and are managed by the Hotel. The laundry hired four or five young women a while back. They were well mannered nice-looking young ladies. No one saw much of them. It seems the laundry had an older woman sort of chaperoning them all the time. I don't know anyone who actually got to know any of them, but there was some trouble from a couple of disrespectful men bothering them. The deputy sheriff broke it up and insisted the women leave town. Said they were too young and an 'attractive nuisance'. A Magistrate from Miles City was passing through and took the women with him over to Miles where they had a better chance of being safe working. The laundry now uses Chinese labors. There are a few women, prostitutes, staying above the hotel, but the Sheriff makes sure they are all older women. If your sister ever arrived here, there is a good chance she was among those who went to Miles City with the Magistrate."

The information both disturbed me, and encouraged me at the same time. If Julie was still alive, she could indeed have been one of the girls Mr. Teel spoke of. Julie could be in Miles City.

I looked up at Mr. Teel, causing him to retort, "I know what you are going to ask. No, I never met any of the girls and I don't know what any of them looked like. Probably only the deputy sheriff would know that, and if I were you, I wouldn't be asking him any questions and attracting attention to yourself. It would be better to listen around to conversations of the workers. Maybe you will learn something of value."

I was bursting to ask one more question. "How do people from here get to Miles City."

He looked at me, and for a change a happier expression graced his face. "Up until now, most people took the stage. That costs a fair bit of money. But the railroad is just a short distance to the east. There's no passenger service yet, but a supply train runs at least three times a week or more if they're working in the flat. In fact, the stage folks are worried that we will soon take away all their business. After you've worked for us a few days, I can get you on the supply train and you can ride free all the way to Miles. In fact, I'm thinking of moving my wife from Glendive to Miles City. Both are important stations for our railroad. We will be shipping a lot of cattle out of there as soon as the bridge across the Missouri is completed. When we get this bridge done and the rails to Livingston, I hope to be able to make the trip back more often myself.”

“That’s great information. Thank your Sir.”

“Well kid, you’ve had a long day.” Reaching into his pocket he pulled out a coin and said, “Here’s two bits. Why don’t you go over to the hotel and get yourself some supper? You can ink out this letter in the morning.”

I thanked him and left. I was happy with the information, but was considerably more desperate to travel to Miles City than he anticipated. I would have to work on an early passage. Somehow, I must find an excuse.

CHAPTER 12   THE COWBOY

After dining on a bowl of soup and a thick sandwich, I picked my way along the frozen path back to the cluster of shelters. The men were gathered in temporary huts for several yards winding down toward the river. Most were waiting, and checking daily, for their names to be posted on the railroad office wall. Both Eddy and Jim were there, along with several others who were camping nearby.

Eddy gave me a friendly greeting as always. Jim looked but said nothing. Intuition told me I should not return to camp and boast about my accomplishment to many who have been waiting in frigid poverty for days before my arrival. A small fire had been built near the open front of our shelter. I stopped at the edge of the containing stones and warmed my hands.

Eddy asked the expected question, "What you been doing? Where you been all day?"

Before I could say anything, one of the newcomers said, "Hey, you're the kid working in the Railroad Office taking names for jobs."

Eddy looked astounded, while others gaped. After several other outsider comments, Eddy simply said, "What?"

I gave a very short explanation, mostly that I just happened to enter the office at a time they needed a person who could read, write and do arithmetic.

A tough looking cowboy who had been sitting on my cowhide hissed, "Well ain't that just real sweet. I've been here freezing my nuts for days while junior here walks in and steals a nice warm office job. Who asked you into camp anyway?"

No one said anything although several seemed to share the same sentiment. Others nodded at me icily. Neither Eddy or Jim spoke in my defense. Outnumbered, I said nothing.

The cowboy got up from his resting position on my hide. He picked it up and placed it over his shoulder saying, "Well, office boy, I guess you won't be needing this." He stepped back indicating he was taking the hide with him.

"Hey, that's mine!", I exclaimed.

"It's mine now."

"It is not. Put it back."

"Maybe I won't, and just kick your ass instead."

"That's mine! I brought it here with me! I need it and you have no right to take it!"

"You know, that's what I'm gonna do Junior. I'm gonna kick your ass!"

Clearly hearing the threat, I turned to face him directly, standing with my hands at my side. To my surprise he struck me squarely in the temple, knocking me to the ground. Stunned, I got up to face him again, only to have him slug me on my left cheek bone, again causing me to fall to the ground.

After the second blow it took me longer to regain my senses. I only half recovered to find the cowboy straddling my chest, pinning my arms to the frozen ground. As he was about to strike me again, I saw a foot swing under the cowboy's throat knocking him backwards. Two more strong kicks from Eddy propelled the cowboy's body off of mine. If any part of the Cowboy's throat remained, it wasn't going to be Eddy's fault.

Several others witnessing the spectacle joined in to break up the scuffle and pulled Eddy away, saving the cowboy from complete destruction. I was only suffering bruises to the face but several of the cowboy's companions seemed to be seriously concerned about his condition. He was retching with severe coughing, spitting blood and unable to speak. The kick to the throat was going to have a lasting effect. He was taken away by his friends.

Eddy put me down on my "precious" cowhide, and began to pelt me with questions.

"What's wrong with you? You trying to get yourself killed? Didn't you see that coming? What were you thinking? Why did you just stand there facing him with your arms down when he said he was going to kick your ass?"

"Eddy, I've never been around anyone like that before. When he said he was going to kick my ass, I thought he meant he was going to plant his boot on my buttocks. I turned my butt away from him so that he couldn't kick it. He said nothing about striking my face."

Eddy held his hands to his face and groaned. "Bub, what are we gonna do with you?"

"Bub, I got to tell you a few things about people."

With pelted speech, Eddy began a lecture that lasted into the night. Some of the lessons I recalled through the pain were:

"When a stranger tells you he is your friend, don't believe him until he proves it. Most likely he wants you for something you've got or something he needs. Never loan a stranger anything. Never tell a stranger anything he asks about you. Don't ever tell anyone anything that won't do you no good. Sleep next to your gun in the dark. Never pay the first price asked for anything you buy. Offer half of what it's worth and bargain from there. If a trader tells you it's his best horse, pass it up, it will have worms or often get the heaves. If the trader says you're lucky and are buying the very last one of something he has for a high price, pass it up because he has several more hidden away that he can't get rid of. Watch to see if the cook eats his own food before you dig in. Don't always volunteer to do the hard jobs because the boss will make a habit of giving them to you. Stay away from women because they will cost you more than you make.

There were many other recommendations, too many to recall. However, when he mentioned women, it brought to mind a word Mr. Teel had used that I did not understand.

After Eddy's display of worldly knowledge, I inquired, "Today I heard a new word. What's a prostitute?"

Eddy broke out in Laughter, rolling off the edge of the cowhide. But before he could answer, a very large man who appeared wearing a deputy sheriff star on his chest commanded, "OK, fellers, stand up."

The deputy was brief. "I understand there's been a fight here and a man's been hurt pretty bad." Looking at me he continued, "You look like you might have been involved as well as your friend there who's supposed to have done the damage."

As I stood and stepped away from the shelter, the deputy spoke again. "And I understand you got a branded cowhide that most likely comes from a stolen cow. I'll be taking that hide and you two fellers with me up to my little office and we'll have a talk about it."

Eddy glanced at me, pursed his lips tightly giving me a sign to keep my mouth shut and say nothing.

As the deputy picked up the hide, he uncovered the rifle. He asked me, "This yours?" I nodded, and he said, "We better take that too."

The walk up to what the deputy called his office was very quiet. The deputy spoke not at all, and stayed two steps behind keeping us in full view. I thought it wise to follow Eddy's advice and also kept silent. The office turned out to be a makeshift jail. The structure was a skeleton of a wood frame covered with canvas, making it no more than a very sturdy tent. It was on the edge of town allowing us to enter without being seen by the curious bar and hotel guests.

As we approached the jail, the deputy opened the door and I could see three jail cells, two of them empty. The compartments more resembled human dog houses than living spaces and were obviously intended for temporary holding cells. He placed my rifle into a gun case and locked a steel bar across the gun frame. He tossed the cowhide against the wall near a battered old desk. Without sitting down, he called to another officer behind a hanging curtain beyond the jail cells.

"Hey Bernie, you want to take one of these fellers and get his story?"

A gray haired balding older man joined us, but was directed to, "Take this feller Eddy that we already know back and see what he says. I'll talk to the kid."

Now I was alone with the deputy that Mr. Teel warned me to avoid because everyone was afraid of him for being very dogmatic. According to Mr. Teel, the town did not have a permanent traditional jail, because Deputy John was known to beat up all offenders to the point that they were quite unwilling to misbehave again.

He began slowly with a fatherly tone. "My name's John, and I'm the Sheriff around here. I don't like trouble, and fights are trouble. The reason they're trouble is that people usually get hurt. Now a feller got hurt tonight and I want you to tell me how that happened."

It sounded like a reasonable request to me and I was happy to explain how I misunderstood a man's intentions when he said he was going to kick my ass. The Deputy, John, looked at me a little curious when I began my story, and appeared even more puzzled as I continued.

"You see Sir, I've never been to a real school, and never been in a fight before. I never even had another boy within miles to play with. So, when he said he was going to kick my ass, I thought he meant with his foot and was surprised when he landed a blow to my head. Eddy saved me from a real beating."

But the dialogue got more difficult when he asked the next question.

"Why'd this cowboy want to kick your ass?"

"I'm not sure. It may be because I just got a job with the railroad and he is still waiting to get on, and because I wouldn't let him steal my cowhide."

"Whoa, now wait a minute, let's take this one at a time. You got a job with the railroad? How old are you?"

It became quickly evident that Mr. Teel was correct, prompting me to follow his advice. "I am sixteen Sir."

"That what you told them?"

"Yes Sir?"

"Have any papers to prove it?"

"No Sir, I was born at home up in the Musselshell Basin."

"Open your mouth!"

"What?"

"Open your mouth, wide!"

I opened my mouth and stuck out my tongue. Deputy John said, "I didn't say stick out your damn tongue, I want to see your teeth!"

After looking he frowned and growled, "You don't look a day past fifteen. But now tell me about this cowhide. The Circle X is a big spread north of here. Drovers bring Long Horns up from Texas; cross through the bottom of the ranch and too often take a few Circle X cattle with them. But they don't often skin the hide off the cow 'cause cows don't sell too good that way. Montana Territory has laws controlling hides with brands on them. That hide is in real good shape, so how did you get it."

Just as if Pa was sitting on my shoulder, I could hear him telling me, "The truth will serve you better than a lie."

My explanation began with the wagon overturning on Pa. I described Wolf, the cave, the winter blizzard and the accidental shooting of the cow. I related how the hide kept me from freezing and the meat from starving, and said as soon as I could earn the money, I intended to repay the Circle X for the cow. I left out everything about Morgan, and how I got to Coulson.

John quietly stared at me with what seemed to be a sympathetic expression. When I finished, he stood up and walked around the room, circling it two or more times. When he sat down, he asked, "That's one hell of a story. Can you prove any single part of that?"

Without hesitating I answered, "Yes Sir, it's a long walk, but I can take you to the busted-up wagon, and to Pa's grave, and the Wolf cave where I shot the cow is just about two miles to the west of that."

I threw in the word walk as a diversion from the horse I rode to town.

John looked at me again and said, "OK kid, I believe you, but I don't believe you are sixteen. Now I have to decide what to do with you. Now you killed and ate a cow that wasn't yours. That's the same as stealing it, and that according to Territory Law is rustling. Now I could hang you, to teach you a lesson, but if I did the lesson would be lost, meaning you wouldn't get much good out of it. But if I turn you loose, you might go out tomorrow and do it again, plus we can't just let cattle rustlers run around unpunished. Because you can't prove you're sixteen and don't look like it, I'm going to turn you over to some people who will look after you until someone will take you into foster care. Lucky for you they will be coming through here first thing day after tomorrow. That means you will stay here in jail until we can get you out to the stage that goes to Twin Bridges. In Twin Bridges they will figure out what to do with you.

I was speechless. He said I was going to stay in jail and be shipped out like a steer to someplace called Twin Bridges? That was going to be completely inhuman.

Deputy John took me by the arm, escorted me into the jail cell, closed the door and turned the key. Once on the outside he looked back to say, "I take it that your only property is that rifle. The hide isn't yours, in spite of the fight for it where a cowboy nearly got killed. I'll get you a blanket cause it gets cold in here at night."

The cell was small and dark, only long enough to hang a three-foot-wide slab for a cowboy bunk on one side. On a dirt floor in an opposite corner sat a bucket, which obviously by its odor, was the toilet. The width of the cell only allowed an occupant to stretch his arms fully open, from one side to the other. To make matters worse, the third cell at the end of the jail was occupied by a mad man who frequently erupted in shouts of profanity and incoherent language.

A little later, Eddy was brought back and placed into the cell next to me. He was not his usual self. His ruddy smile was gone, his eyes dimmed as he stared down at the floor. I knew not to inquire of him at the moment.

We passed several hours in silence. I tried to sleep but I couldn't. I felt responsible for Eddy's presence, but wondered what was meant when John told the other deputy to take Eddy because they already knew him. I kept hearing that statement in my mind until I finally whispered, "Eddy?"

"Yes."

"Are we alone in here?"

"Yes, the Sheriffs gone."

"How come they knew you?"

"'Cause I already got in a fight a few weeks ago."

"Why?"

"Same thing. Somebody was roughing up people that didn't deserve it. I got into it, and got blamed for starting the whole thing. It's not true, but somebody has to say so."

"I told them that the Cowboy started it, and that you saved me from getting really beat up."

"Yeah, well thanks. But now with two fights on my card they're gonna take me before a judge."

"Really, what for?"

"Just a hearing. They'll take me to Miles City when the stage comes through day after tomorrow. Nothing to worry about. What are they going to do with you? How's your head."

"It's OK, but he said I was getting shipped to Twin Bridges to a foster home. Let's talk about this in the morning, because my head actually really is hurting."

Eddy paused, "We may not be able to. The Deputies will probably be back and they don't like prisoners talking among themselves."

"Are we prisoners?"

"These cages aren't for zoo animals. They're keeping us here till they can do something with us. But they won't keep us here long because they don't want to feed or take care of us, and they need the jail space for drunks and fights much worse than ours. The cages aren't strong enough to keep a strong man for very long so the deputy usually beats them up and puts them out of town. We'll be gone in a couple of days. I just have to figure out how to get us out of here."

"What do you mean, you get us out of here? Surely you don't think we can escape."

"No, I don't mean that, but I have an idea. We need Jim to make it work. He should come by in the morning. He always checks in on me. We take care of each other. When he comes by, I'll talk to him. If the deputy is close enough to hear us, you make lots of racket so he doesn't catch our conversation. You have the cell with the window flap. The last time I was in here, that opened up just a little. Does it still open about six inches?"

I stood up on the bunk and slid a board covering a small window. It left an opening about as wide as my spread open hand. I closed it, sat back onto my bunk and whispered, "Yes, it opens clear to the outside."

Eddy only chuckled, "Good, we may need that tomorrow."

Eddy turned his face to the wall in his bunk and said nothing more. I sat in the dim light of the cell, an oil lantern flickering low out on the entry desk. I wanted to cry, but only uneven sobs inhabited my chest. Now this, just when I thought I had somewhere to go.

In deep despair, memories of Ma and Pa haunted me. Again, my mind began comparing my past with the present, while fearing the future. So much I did not understand. How could it be that in a short few days I had again become a thief, a fighter, a cattle rustler, a liar and now in jail? Only I knew that none of these labels belonged to me. What was becoming real to my understanding was that I was not ready to begin living among people. How could they be so false, so two sided, so complicated? Mr. Teel, I admired, but he still frightened and confused me. He spoke very angrily to High Voice, but in turn was very nice to me. I understood Wolf. He would have killed me if I would have given him the chance. But because I did not kill him, he let me live. We tolerated each other on a fair basis, eventually bonded, and because I helped him live with food, he helped me live beyond Morgan. The cowboy attacked me for no reason. He said he was going to kick me, but then struck me. The blood the Cowboy was spitting was of his own causing; had it not been for Eddy it would have been me who was spitting blood. We should no more be punished than Wolf should be shot for his actions. The confusion of it all makes me want to run away, to escape this madness, to run from people, back to the cave and live with the animals.

My thoughts continued between Eddy and Ma and Pa. It could be that Eddy was suffering from a similar illness, less than the madman in the far cell, but from a delusion that we could somehow escape from this jail and live happily ever after. But what about Ma and Pa. Perhaps their search for their fortune in the West was in honesty a disguised escape from St. Louis. Ma said her parents did not approve of Pa. She was not allowed to sit at the dinner table with Pa's family. They left comfort in St. Louis to be free, in a place where they could be themselves. They loved each other, and the freedom of the wild wilderness. They loved it in spite of the hardships and loved it to death – theirs. Perhaps their plan involved more than I realized.

CHAPTER 13   THE PLAN

One deputy, the old one, arrived with the morning sun. He brought the first real breakfast I experienced in a long time. He checked to see that we were both alive, but spoke little. When we finished eating, he took the tin plates and left the jail. Eddy and I were free to talk.

I was awake most of the night with a throbbing head, and thinking about whatever Eddy was planning. I reasoned that whatever was waiting for me in Twin Bridges surely would not be worse than the punishment I would receive if I were caught breaking out of jail. I was surprised Eddy would be thinking so radically. The words of his own lecture reminded me not to trust a stranger with an unusual circumstance. However, I was most disturbed that I would not be showing up for my new job on the very second day of employment. What would Mr. Teel think? He was a nice man and I felt great shame in letting him down. I couldn't wait any longer, I had to probe Eddy's thoughts.

"Eddy, what are we going to do?"

"OK Bub, here's just part of the plan. They are going to send you to Twin Bridges, and me to Miles City. But you would rather go to Miles City, wouldn't you?"

"Well sure, but how would that work out? What are they going to do with you?"

"I'll just have to go to a hearing. That's a meeting when you go in front of a Judge and tell him what went wrong and he decides what to do. In my case, I was just protecting somebody, so he will give me a lecture and turn me loose. Now that could be me, or it could be you."

"Wow, I don't know."

"In your case they are gonna take you to somebody who thinks they can tell you everything you should do for another year or at least until somebody thinks you are sixteen. They might work you for that year or whip you if you don't work. And don't think they will be paying you or feeding you eggs and pancakes every morning. There will be some old codgers there to make you miserable every day until you wish you were back in the cave in the hills. But if I go there in your place, I could arrive, tell them there's been a big mistake and walk away."

"What will they do to me if they find out I'm not you?"

"Well if they don't have bad things planned for me, you go free, if they want to punish me, you do the same thing. Tell them the deputies made a big mistake by transporting us to the wrong places and we both go free. Remember, if you're sixteen, and you haven't done anything the Judge in Miles City won't have anything to keep you for."

"OK, so what would cause the deputies to make this terrible mistake?"

"I can't fit into your clothes, but you can fit into mine. See, Jim and I got lucky and found some clothes that fell out of a wagon near the trader's store at Huntley. We got several pants and shirts all the same. We hid them under a rain barrel in town. I'll have Jim get you pants and shirt just like mine. You need some new clothes anyway. If the deputy will let you put them on today fine, if not we'll slip them through the window tonight. We will both look the same in the morning. They'll be here before dawn."

Eddy was getting more excited as he talked, and his enthusiasm was spreading to me. But a few of his statements bothered me and left some concern. They came from his own lessons.

"Wait a minute Eddy. How did matching clothes fall out of a wagon in Huntley twenty miles from here, and you just happened to pick them up? That sounds just too fantastic."

"OK, one of the things I didn't mention is that the word fantastic is just a charm school word for bullshit. Now I know you never use it, and may not understand it, but it means just what it sounds like; bullshit. So, what do you care if we broke into the trading post and stole some clothes?"

"What do you mean, what do I care?", I said a little too loudly, "I'm not wearing any stolen clothes!"

"Shush!" Eddy said in hushed breath. "Look Bub. Either we are getting out of here or we aren't and you have to go along with the plan. Consider the clothes a gift from Jim and me and forget about the rest of the 'fantastic'.

He continued, "Look here at this back wall. The board next to the bar pushes back into the wall."

Eddy put his shoulder against the wall and bent the vertical board away from the cell wall far enough to demonstrate.

"You can push it back far enough to force through from one cell to another. I discovered that the last time I was here. Tonight, we can change places. When the deputies come to get us, pretend to be sleepy, let them put us on the wrong stages and we're out of here on their stupid mistake. I'll go to Twin Bridges and you'll go to Miles city. We play dumb until we arrive and they will all want to get rid of us and cover up their stupidity."

"Eddy, that sounds really risky. Couldn't we get into bigger trouble?"

"Why? We aren't breaking any laws. Just play along, and they can't punish you for being stupid."

Again, I thought of Ma and Pa. I mentally relived the risks they had taken to be able to make their own choices. I finally understood why they never gave up. There was a choice to be made; a risky one. Let fools and circumstances run my life, or struggle free. Eddy was offering a sure ride to Miles City. They would probably feed me on the way.

"OK, let's do it."

Just as Eddy promised, Jim appeared about noon as the deputy was pre-occupied with his own lunch. Jim was given a quick search and left alone to visit with Eddy. After receiving his instructions Jim soon returned with a shirt and pants the same as Eddy's, but in the meantime had changed out of his similar getup into older worn garments. Eddy was clever. At least there was not going to be three of us looking exactly the same.

This time the deputy was more concerned with what Jim was bringing into the jail. He searched the shirt and pants and asked, "What do they need these for?"

Jim smoothly said, "He will be going to meet new people and he should be better dressed."

The deputy looked over at me, shrugged his shoulders and tossed the clothing into my cell, saying, "Throw the dirty ones outside when you're changed."

I put the new Levi Strauss pants and shirt on. The pants were a little long, but looked far better than the short, frayed cottons I had been wearing for months. The shirt was stiff, but I felt quite stylish.

Eddy said, "Great, we look almost alike. Now give me your hat."

Pa's coat was spread out on the dirt floor in my cell, the hat resting on the back shoulder. Heavy dark tan material, felt or beaver, I didn't know, composed its oval body. A flat crown was faded and slightly stained, bearing irregular pinch marks in the front from the many grasps of Pa's thumb and forefinger. Around the outside of the crown a leather band only partly covered a hilly landscape of salt and sweat, while the wide tired brim spoke of its history in the wilderness.

I paused. An image of Pa wearing that hat passed through my mind. I saw him fixing the corral fence in the bright sun; under that hat. He bent into the rain herding our few cattle; in that hat. Just before he died, I saw him riding the wagon pulling on Old Billy's reins; in that hat. With him fresh in the grave, I stood up and walked away; under that hat.

I looked at Eddy firmly and said "No!"

"What?"

"I'm not giving you this hat! It's my Pa's hat and it's the only thing I have left of his and I'm taking it with me."

"But for Hell's sake Bub, that's the most noticeable thing about you. I can't look like you without that hat."

"I don't care, the hat stays with me."

"Bub, your Pa's dead! It's just a piece of felt. I need it on my head to get out of here. I can't believe you are going to let a damn hat bust up this whole plan."

"Look Eddy, my Pa's gone, at least he isn't here this minute. But he still lives here sometimes under this hat, here in my head. And sometimes he comes out and sits on my shoulders and I still learn from things he said a long time ago. And when I wear this hat my Ma sees me in it and loves me just as she did him. They both died so I could be alive today, and I am going to walk out of this damn cattle pen under this hat, and nobody trying to kick my ass is going to keep me from it."

Eddy sat there blinking as if I smacked him in the forehead. "Well, OK Bub, but would you at least carry it out in your hand when we walk outa here?"

"Sure. You said it would still be dark anyway."

When it was dark, and the entire town was quiet, Eddy whispered, "OK Bub, it's time to do the big switch."

Eddy was strong, and put his shoulder to the back wall. The boards creaked and bent outward away from the vertical iron bars separating the two cells. The space he created was just wide enough to allow his muscular body to squeeze past into my cell. Standing next to me, he put his hand on my back and whispered, "Your turn Bub."

I was not as strong as Eddy, but also not as broad and muscular. I slid through the space with ease.

Eddy giggled, saying, "Now you is me, and I is you. You sure you don't want to part with this hat?

In fright, I replied, "No, I forgot it over there and if you don't give it over here to me, I'll scrap this whole thing."

"Don't get excited Bub, I was just kidding you," Eddy said as he handed the hat and coat through the bars.

"This is no time for kidding Eddy. I can't ever remember being as scared as I am right now. I've made some bad mistakes but I've never done anything really bad before, and I can't decide if this is a mistake, or bad, or a bad mistake."

CHAPTER 14   ESCAPE

The deputy, the one called Bernie, came early. Eddy was right. It was still dark.

Bernie grumbled, "Get your asses out of bed, the stages leave here at five sharp and one of you is gonna be on each one of them. The way he emphasized the word each indicated he had his instructions clear.

I gathered up my only belongings which were Pa's hat and coat. Our coats were similar, satisfying Eddy that they need not be exchanged. I followed his orders, and discretely kept the hat concealed under the coat as Bernie let me out of the cell. I was too terrified to talk, but Eddy, contrary to his usual demeanor when in trouble, was quite talkative. Twice he made a point of speaking to me, the first time which was quite startling.

He said, "Hey Eddie, how come they let you out first?"

When I realized he was just beginning his clever charade, pretending to be me, I could still only squeeze out a mild, "I don't know."

Bernie walked us to the stage stop. Both coaches were waiting; one facing west, and one to the east.

The two drivers were waiting on the ground talking about their routes and settling in the other passengers. Because Coulson was the starting point of these routes, only one passenger was in the east bound coach and two in for the western route.

Eddy did not wait to be guided to his place in the western coach. He stepped up to the door, turned and waved to me saying, "So long Eddy, maybe I'll see you in about a year."

A terrible lump in my throat kept me from answering, while at the same time, Bernie took my arm and pushed me into the other coach. However, he did not close the door. He spoke to the driver saying, "This is Eddy. He's ready now."

The driver came to the coach door. He reached into the side of the coach and pulled up a length of chain. With practiced dexterity, he wrapped the chain around my lower leg and locked the chain to the sidewall of the coach.

Bernie backed away from the stage saying, "He's all yours now."

Within two revolutions of the big stage coach wheels, I knew I had been struck again. This time by Eddy.

My immediate thought was to start screaming, but I learned from Pa to think things through completely before acting. Eddy was a rascal, but he wasn't stupid. Did he just use me unmercifully, or did he leave me an avenue of escape by thinking on my own from this point forward? The major objective I could accomplish was getting to Miles City. Once there I would have to transform back into Tobias

Hawthorn, a God fearing lying sixteen-year-old. I decided to ride it out.

The stage driver was quite stern at first, but when I was continually polite to him, he began to respond accordingly. We stopped occasionally for passenger relief, and to change horses at various stage stops. During each stop I was unchained and allowed to walk freely among the other travelers. After the second stop I noticed that the chain around my leg was looped in a manner that would allow me to slide it down around my boot. From there it was an easy feat to slip my foot out of Pa's oversized boot and extract it from the chain. I practiced it a couple of times while the other passengers were asleep, always returning my foot back into its captivity.

I contemplated freeing myself and leaping from the door, rolling to my feet and fleeing off into the sage and pines. Had I not already had the experience of living in a similar environment I might have tried it. But reality stifled the fantasy and I let the chain remain.

As night began to cover us, I realized we were rumbling along beside railroad tracks. Through the window of the moving stage coach, I caught my first glimpse of a railroad. To my surprise, the stage stopped at a small building beside the tracks and all passengers got out.

The driver hopped off his lofty perch, unchained me, and said, "This is as far as I go."

I asked, "Is this Miles City?"

"No, not for another seventy miles or so. From here they're gonna put you on to the work train."

"The work train?"

"Yup, from here the work train runs at night, back to Miles City. It's got a car that's half mail car, and half passenger car. You'll be riding in there tonight."

The driver looked around the crowded platform, and whistled at another man wearing a lawman's star. The deputy walked to the coach and was told, "Here's your man from Coulson that is supposed to go on to Miles City. The sheriff over at Coulson says he has a court appearance sometime tomorrow, and they want him on the night train."

The deputy appeared to know nothing about me or anything more than what he was just told. The fewer questions I had to answer, the better I felt. I spoke not a word.

Once again, I was escorted to my next ride by a law man. I was excited to receive my first train ride, but would rather have it under different circumstances. I was taken to the rear of the eleven-car train, where I was directed to climb a couple of short steps into a box car which had been divided into two sections. The section I entered had seats for passengers, while the other had two desks and several sacks of what looked like mail and other papers.

Before I was seated, a man at one of the desks said, "Sign the manifest over here."

I looked at him puzzled, and he explained, "Everybody that rides, signs the passenger sheet so we know who and how many are riding the train. If you can't write, put you mark on the line anyway."

My pulse quickened. I recognized this as a defining point where I openly participated in a fraud, or boldly claimed my innocence. I sensed there was much more waiting for me in Miles City than Eddy indicated, and whatever this "Hearing" thing was going to be had lawmen guarding me as if I were likely to escape if given the chance. This was my chance to reinvent myself.

I walked up to the desk, palmed the paper and moved it to rest squarely before me while the railroad man watched. I took his pen and in very large writing, covering two lines instead of the usual one, I wrote Tobias Hawthorn. The railroad man took notice of the large signature, but said nothing. The deputy languished in the archway oblivious of what had occurred. As I stepped into the passenger car, the deputy stopped me, saying, "You won't be riding in here. Your place is back here in the baggage compartment."

With that he produced a familiar looking length of chain, wrapped it in the same sloppy fashion as before, locked the chain to the boxcar sidewall and tossed the key to the railroad attendant. As the deputy departed, he instructed the attendant that I would be met by someone from the court in Miles City. The attendant glanced at me, then at the key, and left it lying on his desk.

My first train ride was a serious let down. I could see nothing from my baggage car confinement. The motion of the car was every bit as bad as the stage coach, but was slightly less breezy. The baggage clerk worked silently beside me, sorting mail and other boxes and writing messages that I didn't understand. I was quite uncomfortable, and as I kept turning in search of a reasonable position, he looked at me and pointed at the chain.

"Is that necessary?" he asked.

"No", I responded as I pushed the chain down around my boot top and removed the boot from my foot. To heighten his amazement, I shook the chain off of my boot and reinserted my foot. I smiled at him, stretched out on the mail sacks and advised, "Don't worry, I'm not going anywhere. I want to get to Miles City."

We stopped several times but I had no view of anything other than mail and baggage moving in and out of my car. Generally, the train car kept rocking through the night. It seemed to have a purpose. I slept for more than I had in two days.

CHAPTER 15   THE ACTOR

I was up, sitting on the baggage clerk's desk when the Miles City deputy entered the railroad car. This time he asked for the "Passenger from Coulson", but only made the audible inquiry into the baggage car. He seemed a little startled to see me sitting on the desk, legs hanging over the side, both boots on, and the humiliating chain crumpled along the wall. I looked up to say good morning, but the clerk was quicker to respond, nodding in my direction, "There's your man."

I knew that now the world was my stage, and the curtain just got opened. I hopped off the desk, held out my hand to the deputy and said, "Good morning Sir. I'm Tobias Hawthorn."

The deputy stopped stone still where he stood. He didn't offer his hand and said, "And you're also known as Eddy Kingston, right?"

"No Sir, never have been. They mostly call me Toby, but never Eddy."

The deputy declined to provide his name, flexed the muscles in his jaw, and said, "We'll see about this. Come with me."

For the first time in three days, I wasn't either pulled by the arm or watched like a runaway bronc. I followed the deputy at a quick pace to a buggy tied at the end of the train platform.

I had learned that keeping quiet was a precious talent if used at the right time. I spoke not a word unless the deputy made an inquiry, which he did not while we rode into the middle of town. The frozen buggy ruts jarred me into the realization that prior to a few moments ago, I had never known Eddy's full name. Eddy Kingston; I couldn't help wondering where they got his name, or if it even was his true name. To me, he was just Eddy, a person whom I have yet to identify; as a friend or a trickster to avoid.

At a building still under construction, the deputy drove the horses around to the back and tied them so the buggy was protected from the busy street. Two signs were prominently displayed, nailed above a doorway. The larger sign spelled "Court House", the other smaller one contained only four letters, J-a-i-l.

I was led inside where two other deputies were apparently attending to the jail. One took me aside, and searched my pockets, boots and anywhere else I might have something useful. When they were finished examining me, the second began asking me questions. With each answer they appeared to become more confused.

I gave them my true name, added one year to my age, told them about Ma and Pa and the Musselshell. They frequently looked at each other, sometimes asking me to repeat my answers.

The final question seemed to cause the most consternation. The older deputy of the two asked, "Now tell me son, why are you here?"

"As best as I can figure sir, Deputy John in Coulson didn't like my teeth."

The entire room fell into dead silence. Finally, with twice the volume he shrieked, "He didn't like your what?"

Eddy told me to act a little stupid, and I had seen plenty of stupid in the last week. This was still my stage so I carried on.

"I got a job with the railroad in Coulson. A cowboy there got mad at me because he wanted a job and didn't get one. He was kicking my ass when this guy Eddy stopped him. The cowboy hurt me, and Eddy hurt the cowboy and the sheriff took Eddy and me to the jail. The sheriff knew I didn't do nothing wrong, but he don't like kids in town. I explained I was sixteen, and proved it to the railroad, but the deputy didn't believe me. He made me show him my teeth, gave me hell for sticking out my tongue, and said he didn't believe I was more than fifteen, so he sent me out of town. I thought I was going' someplace else, but ended up here."

Everyone in the jail looked at me with amazement. I could tell I did a good job of acting, something I had never done before.

"And you swear you are not Eddy Kingston?"

"No Sir, I mean yes Sir, I swear it. I didn't even know Eddy's name until just when you said it in here."

I thought it was time to take my chances and learn what I was scheduled to face.

"Why, what's Eddy done that you want him here?"

The older deputy answered, "Charges have been filed against Eddy Kingston for two counts of assault and battery and one charge of sexual assault."

I looked at all of them, half acting and half sincere, "What's that mean?"

"It means that whoever Eddy is, you or somebody else, beat or battered up a couple of men, and also attacked a female. All of this occurred in Coulson in the last three months."

"Well Sir, that wasn't me because I just got into Coulson on March 10th the day before my sixteenth birthday, so I wasn't even there then. I got the railroad job on March 11th and that's when me and the cowboy got hurt." I knew I was using bad grammar, but it was part of the act.

The talkative older deputy scratched his chin, and said, "OK, Eddy, err- Toby, we'll have to figure this out. You are due in court this afternoon, but the judge is going to want to know what's going on here. Maybe we'll just let him figure it out. In the meantime, if I had a nickel for every bugger that lied to me, I would own the railroad. We're going to put you into our jail until we can figure out who you are, and why in the hell you are in Miles City."

They escorted me into the next room, a long hall containing eight jail cells on one side. I was placed in the first one. A little disheartened, I wasn't sure how

I was going to convince them I was Toby, but I knew they could not prove I was Eddy. At the top of my thoughts was "sexual assault". What was that all about?

The Miles City jail was less primitive than the temporary cages in Coulson. My feet were resting on a wooden plank floor. A covered chamber pot was partially hidden under a thinly padded bunk. Clean folded blankets placed at the foot of the bunk made the place look less hostile. I could hear sounds of wagons and horses from the street. Still unaccustomed to being a jail cell inhabitant, I wondered how long this was going to take.

Although I was consumed with my own fate, I could not put Julie from the forefront of my thoughts. The new shirt Eddy had given me was stiff and scratchy at the collar. The irritation was making the skin around my neck sore, and I realized why many cowboys wore a scarf or bandana of some sort around their neck. With each scratch, the itchy irritation reminded me of Julie's scarf, and of its discovery on Morgan. With renewed anxiety I vowed to resume my quest to find her, hopefully alive.

By late afternoon I began to think I was not going to be taken before this judge for whom I had traveled so far. As if to answer my thoughts, the older deputy whom I had heard referred to as Cal, approached my cell.

In an apologetic tone he explained, "Toby, there have been some complications that we are attempting to resolve. Judge Adams will not see you today, but should see you in the morning. It appears you will be represented by counsel."

I tried to ask additional questions, but he turned away saying only, "That's all I can tell you. We'll bring you in supper shortly."

But I found it encouraging that he called me Toby.

I spent much of the night worrying about counsel. What did that involve? I knew that in the Bible they had councils where groups got together to decide things. Maybe they were going to have a big meeting to evaluate my story. Did I dare play stupid in front of several people, maybe many who would be smart enough to judge my falsity? But Ma also talked about people in St. Louis who were lawyers; people who studied laws and helped other people understand them. But lawyers traded advice for money. No such person would give his time to assist an urchin of my stature.

I mused, "Again, I will have to wait in suspense. Life is so strange. It moves in lightning fast leaps, leaving you unprepared, dumfounded with the unknown, and then stalls to torture, with illusions and fears of dire forthcomings."

With the rising sun, I begged a cup of water from the night jailer. I drank it and begged another. With the second, I wet the end of my shirttail and brushed away as many soiled spots from my shirt and jeans as possible. I even cleaned up Pa's hat. The jailer observed my actions, seemed amused and provided a cloth and towel saying I should continue the job by washing my face and brushing my hair. I finished the job by wiping off my boots. Feeling much refreshed, I sat in my bunk listening to the deputy's conversation. I perked up at the mention of counsel.

A man in a dark pin stripped suit entered the jail and was speaking with Cal. The man carried a tablet sized leather case, wore spectacles, a neck tie pinned in with a button-down collar on his shirt. He placed a fine-looking gentleman style hat on an entry desk and said, "Bring him to me."

Cal opened my cell and said, "Your barrister is here."

I had no idea what he was talking about but knew it must be the man who just entered the jail.

Cal led me to the impressive looking gentleman, who looked at me from eyebrows to knee caps. His first statement was a question.

"Mr. Tobias Hawthorn I assume?"

Pa seemed to be on my shoulder shouting, "Play time is over."

"Yes Sir, may I have the courtesy of your name please?"

The man broke into a friendly smile easing my extreme tension.

"Toby, I am Abraham Lavine. I am a lawyer for the Northern Pacific Railroad. The company has contacted me on your behalf as an employee to represent you in a matter of false arrest, unjust prosecution, mistaken identity and other charges we see fit to bring. Now we are going to appear before Judge Adams in about an hour and I need to know as much as possible about you."

"Yes Sir, but first can you tell me how you know me and how you knew I was here?"

"Oh, yes. You seem to have earned quite a reputation with the railroad folks over in Coulson and all the way back to St. Paul. You apparently demonstrate some worth as an employee, as an author of business prose, and future management abilities. The Head Surveyor, Mr. Teel was disturbed when you failed to report to work on March 12th. He was about to begin inquiries when this Deputy John Johnston strode into Teel's office and admonished him for hiring you as an under aged kid. Teel was offended because he had verified your age and argued with the deputy. Teel said he wanted you back immediately. Old John said it was too late, because he already sent you to someplace that dispenses with orphans. Teel sent a telegram to the stage stop at Bozeman with orders to take you off the stage and return you to Coulson. But when they stopped the stage, a person named Eddy got off and said there had been a mistake, and you were headed for Miles City. Nobody seemed to care about Eddy and he just walked off without telling us anything about you. That confused things a bit until we found on the Miles City work train manifest you had signed your name in big bold letters."

Mr. Lavine continued, "Now I don't want to know how that little error was arranged, or if it even was arranged. But Judge Adams has unsettled charges against Eddy, and he has to be convinced you are not to blame for anything and need to be rightfully returned to your place of employment. We are going to do that, but I don't know what evidence the Judge has against Eddy. He will question you. You must answer truthfully, to the best of your knowledge. But you need not volunteer anything, and it is best not to. Only answer the questions he asks."

He looked at me sternly and said, "Now, to the best of your knowledge you and Mr. Teel understand that you reached your sixteenth birthday on March 11, 1882. Is that right?"

I closed my eyes to Pa on my shoulder and answered, "Yes Sir." I felt like a rat eyed liar, but sensed it would be the only lie I had to tell all day.

After that I provided a synopsis of my life, culminating in the altercation with the cowboy. I also exonerated Eddy, making him a hero for saving me. I thought I owned him that much.

Mr. Lavine smiled and said, "Good, I think we are ready."

He noticed I was looking at him with a questioning expression. He asked, "What is it?"

"They said Eddy was charged with sexual assault. What is that about?"

"I don't know Toby. I'm sure they will have witnesses to something, but as long as we have nothing to do with it, we will not share the concern."

Maybe not, but I had plenty of concern.

CHAPTER 16   TESTIMONY

The courtroom was small; made of the finest wood I had ever seen. The Judge's chair was elevated above the rest of us who sat below in rows on each side of the judge. When he entered we were all told to rise. I watched Mr. Lavine, and only sat down after he did.

Various people took turns speaking and finally Judge Adams said, "Now we will take up the matter of Eddy Kingston, alleged two counts of assault and battery and one count of sexual assault. These charges come from an information from Deputy John Jeremiah Johnston, at Coulson, Montana Territory. Barrister Lavine, do you represent the defendant?"

Mr. Lavine stood up and answered, "No your Honor, I do not represent the defendant."

"Well then what in Heavens are you doing here?"

"Your Honor, this takes some explanation. My client is not Eddy Kingston, but was sent here by Deputy Johnston in error, believing him to be Eddy Kingston."

"Mr. Lavine, I have been on this bench many years and no one has ever appeared before me by error or accident."

Mr. Lavine summarized the events of my circumstances in an eloquent manner, making Deputy Johnston and his staff appear as fools, and me as an unfortunate victim.

At the end of the explanation, Judge Adams exclaimed, "This entire matter is based on hearsay evidence which I am reluctant to even refer to trial. However, we have witnesses here in court that can clear this up. Mr. Hawthorn, please take the stand."

Mr. Lavine had explained what I must do. I moved to the chair next to the Judge and was sworn to tell the truth.

Judge Adams' first statement was, "Please state your name for the record."

"Tobias Hawthorn."

The Judge asked, "Do you know Eddy Kingston?
"Yes Sir."

"Did you start a fight with a cowboy.?"

"No Sir."

"Were you in an altercation with a Cowboy in Coulson?"

"Yes Sir."

"Did this cowboy strike you during this altercation?"

"Yes Sir."

"Did you strike him back?"

"No Sir."

"Why not?'

"I was on the ground Sir."

"Then what did Eddy Kingston do?"

"He knocked the cowboy off of me and kept me from being further hurt."

"How many times did Eddy strike the cowboy?"

"I'm not sure, not more than twice."

I didn't mention kicked, because I reasoned one could honestly say that Eddy's foot struck the cowboy.

"Now will you give me a description of Eddy please."

I described Eddy as best as possible, about my size, less than six feet tall, thin but muscular with sandy hair.

"One more thing Tobias, your Counselor said Deputy Johnston did not believe you were sixteen years of age, and thereafter rendered his own judgment based on an examination of your teeth. Is that right?"

"Yes Sir."

"How did he perform this examination?"

"He made me open my mouth. He looked inside and made me draw back my tongue while he looked."

"And as a result of that examination you were denied the return to your job, were imprisoned and shipped out of town, is that right?"

"Yes Sir"

"You may return to your seat."

As I returned, Mr. Lavine rose and said, "Your Honor, based on the testimony presented, I move that all charges against my client be dismissed."

Judge Adams said sternly, "Not yet Mr. Lavine. We have a few loose ends to tie here. We haven't even established that there are charges against your client, because we haven't ruled in or out who he is for sure. This is the worst mess I have ever been involved in, and I want to get it completely resolved today."

Judge Adams then called a middle-aged woman to be given the oath preceding testimony. Dressed in tired clothing she appeared as a faded flower that had long lost its fragrance. She gave her name as Wilma White.

The Judge began with an explanation. "Mrs. White, I have a report here from Deputy Johnston quoting a woman in Coulson who says three out of four of her female employees were assaulted while they were working at a laundry. However, this woman did not witness the assault. The report mentioned that you were present but it doesn't appear that you or any of the young ladies were questioned. I am at a loss to understand why the victims of an assault were never interviewed; however, we can resolve the issue here. Will you please tell me what happened?"

Wilma responded, "First of all, there were only three girls, not four, and only two of them were assaulted. The girls were outside in back of the laundry washing clothes. We had a large water kettle and an open fire. Two young men approached them and immediately began talking rude and making improper advances. I noticed that they had come from the saloon and assumed they were drunk. I was several yards away when each man grabbed a girl and attempted to drag them toward the back of the laundry building. I screamed and another man who was hauling wood for the fire ran in the direction of the men. He was carrying a chunk of firewood and clubbed both of them solidly about the head. Both were injured and bleeding. One fell down but was helped back up by the other. They ran away toward the transient worker encampment. One of the girls had her dress torn off the shoulder and the other was scratched up a little. The third girl, sort of the leader of the three, had run toward the wood pile and was OK. She kept on running and I lost track of her. She eventually got help and got us out of town before the deputy could punish us. But before that occurred, I knew the deputy would be coming because of all the ruckus. None of the girls working at the laundry that day were sixteen, so I took them with me back to the boarding house. The woman who owned and ran the laundry spoke to the deputy, but she didn't see the incident. She was also my boss and I know her to be a hard person. She would not have given the Deputy John much information about the girls because he would have given her hell for keeping girls that young in town."

Judge Adams rubbed his forehead and asked, "Who was this man who clubbed the other two?"

"I don't know him, but one of the girls said his name was Eddy."

"Could it have been Eddy Kingston?"

"I don't know, everybody just called him Eddy."

"Did this Eddy at any time assault one of the girls?"

"No Sir, he protected them."

"And what brought you to Miles City?"

"Sheriff John caught wind that we were working with girls that were under his preferred age. None of them had living parents and we knew he would send them out of town. We had friends here that said they could use domestic help, so we moved."

"Mrs. White, look at the men in this room. Do you see the person you know as Eddy in this room?"

"No sir."

"I understand you have one of the girls with you today."

"Yes Sir."

"That will be all. You may step down."

The judge turned toward the door and ordered, "Deputy, will you bring the girl in?"

The deputy entered with a slender red haired shy looking girl about the same age as me, and about the same size as Julie would have been. She was sworn in next to the Judge; gave her name as Grace Nelson and began to answer questions. Judge Adams was gentler and briefer with her.

"Do you know a man named Eddy?"

"Yes."

"Do you know his last name?"

"No, they just call him Eddy."

"Is Eddy in this room today."

She looked briefly around the room and answered, "No."

"Is Eddy one of the persons who assaulted you?"

"What does assault mean?"

"Did he put his hands on you and hurt you?"

The girl frowned and replied, "A drunk old fat guy did behind the laundry, but it wasn't Eddy. Eddy ran them off."

The Judge leaned back in his chair and said, "That will be all."

Mr. Lavine rose and said, "Your Honor, I again move that all charges against my client, Tobias Hawthorn be dropped for lack of foundation."

Judge Adams became quite animated and replied, "Your motion is not necessary. I am throwing this whole damn mess out based on pure biased falsehood. In all my years I have never seen such a mess and waste of time. The wrong people are being penalized here. If my jurisdiction were expanded, I would see that certain deputies' wages were docked to compensate this man's loss of wages. If I were to allow a man to be judged by his teeth, the next thing is I would be judged by my lack of hair."

"All charges against Mr. Eddy Kingston are dismissed. There are no charges of record concerning your client Mr. Hawthorn, and I think it honorable that the Northern Pacific Railway has taken upon itself to represent justice in this Territory. Can you make arrangements to accommodate this man's safe trip back to his place of employment, and see that it is continued without prejudice or tarnish?"

"Yes your Honor. I will make arrangements to place him in our company boarding house until the next train leaves to our western most terminal. He shall receive free stage passage to Coulson from there."

"Very good. Court is no longer in session." The judge slammed down a wooden hammer and departed.

CHAPTER 17   MAKEOVER

Mr. Lavine presented me with a handshake and took me outside. He explained that I was still considered an employee of the railroad, and in considering myself so, must behave accordingly. After the formalities of introducing me to official employment, quite differently than what had occurred my first day in Coulson, he laid out my agenda for the rest of the day.

"Toby the Northern Pacific is very interested in developing you as an employee within our administration. Now that strange circumstances have already brought you to our offices here in Miles City, certain members of our staff are interested in meeting you. That will occur tomorrow. I suggest we take the rest of the afternoon to make you, ah, a little more presentable."

"Yes Sir, I did what I could to clean up before court, but these are the only clothes I have, and I had to borrow a towel from the jailer."

"I understand. I have a budget that will allow us to purchase new pants and shirt, and a couple other items to brighten your appearance. Perhaps we can even find a barber to trim our hair."

Of course, I had never been to a clothing store, or a barber before, but I did not tell Mr. Lavine. My silence appeared uncomfortable, and he asked, "Have you ever been to an apparel shop before?"

Not to appear to backward I answered, "My Ma used to own a dress shop in St. Louis, but I've never been there."

The railway and Mr. Lavine were very generous. He purchased me a fine shirt, with red and white squares, and black cotton pants, with a silver buckled belt. The last items were low cut shoes and black socks. It was quite embarrassing to remove my Pa's boots to reveal my bare un-socked feet. The new items were put into a cloth bag after Mr. Lavine suggested I not wear them until I had the opportunity to get a hair trim and a bath. He explained that my room at the boarding house would have a bathing tub.

By the time we entered the barber shop my counselor and I had become quite conversant. He suggested a gentleman's style cut and I, not knowing the distinction between one cut or another, agreed. I caught a brief glimpse in what appeared to be a mirror before the work began, I was so shocked at the undisciplined matted locks, I would have agreed to most suggestions. The barber even suggested he shave the sparse gathering of hair emerging on my lip and chin.

With a prouder posture, I exited the trim parlor with Mr. Lavine. He looked over the remake and said, "I think we need just one more thing. How about a new mildly western hat?"

An answer did not come forth quickly. I could not part with Pa's hat. By now I trusted Mr. Lavine to have a sense of understanding so I elected to tell him the truth, choosing my words carefully.

"I would be proud and grateful to have a new hat Sir. But I cannot discard my present hat because it belonged to my Pa. I have an emotional attachment to it, that allows me to feel a certain presence of Pa when I wear it.

Mr. Lavine stopped walking, and gently put his hand on my shoulder. "Toby, I'm not suggesting you throw away your father's hat any more than I would suggest you erase his memory. But don't you think that your father would be proud to see you dressed like a gentleman, accomplishing great things with your life? You can always cherish his memory with his hat proudly hung by your bedside, or on your office wall. You can keep it ready at hand to wear on special occasions and thereby preserve it for the life of your memories. You won't then allow it to disintegrate from the elements."

I pondered the thought of the wind, tearing Pa from my head and carrying him away into some rushing river, never to be seen again.

"Yes Sir, I think you are right. What do you think would look best, grey or brown?"

The Northern Pacific boarding house was a large three-story structure, with white siding, and black shutters at the side of each window. We walked up its impressive steps into an entry revealing a tall carpeted stairway to the upper floors. A small tall writing desk stood by the doorway. A wrinkled little lady, wearing a net over her grey hair took a position behind the desk. She greeted Mr. Lavine by name, revealing she knew him, and produced a guest book for me to sign.

My generous new savior walked me to an upstairs room and advised he would contact me again in the morning after I had breakfast which would be served here at the company quarters. From the background, the host lady announced that supper would be served in the downstairs dining room at the sound of the dinner bell.

I scarcely noticed the beauty of the room. I had never entered anything so elegant, but the situation presented another dilemma. Somehow, I must stall my return to Coulson until I had learned more about Julie. It was imperative that I meet the management that so generously extracted me from the abyss of trouble I had fallen into, but I could not ignore the thought that Julie could be in a far worse world.

Knowing that supper would be the next hill I must climb, I eagerly filled the bath tub with water and took the first real bath I could ever remember. There was even a comb next to a mirror in the bath area. This lodging was amazing. I donned all of the new clothing with the exception of the new hat. Ma often told me that a proper gentleman never wears his hat in the house and especially not at the dining table. I examined the new Toby in the first mirror I had ever peered into. Julie and I used to examine ourselves in the reflection of smooth water pools down at the creek. But a real glass mirror was just another remarkable experience.

I looked closely at the young man I had been living with all my life, but had never really seen before. He had changed considerably since the reflecting pool. Now, thick wavy brown hair adorned an oval shaped head. Deep set hazel eyes rested in a thin but bold looking face, finished with a strong jaw and square chin. The teeth so closely inspected by Deputy John were straight and white giving credit to Ma's hygiene lectures. I was confident the man I was observing could pass for sixteen any time. But perhaps I should just keep my mouth shut.

I nervously sat in a bedside chair and mentally reviewed the lessons Ma had taught me about proper eating manners. In our Musselshell dugout, Pa had cut a table made of wood slabs. Our table cloth was canvas. We had real spoons and forks that Ma taught me how to hold properly. There were all those words like, "please pass", "thank you", "no thank you", "you're welcome", and "excuse me." In spite of our humble existence, Ma insisted we carry on a "respectable life." This would be the test, and I dare not let her down.

The dinner bell rang, and I stepped down the staircase in my new shoes with great trepidation. I hoped the lump in my throat would not prevent me from swallowing.

CHAPTER 18   SUPPER

The dining table was long with eight chairs on each side. A white linen table cloth lay beneath silver and blue plates. Fresh yellow flowers were cuddled in a matching vase centered among it all.

I took a place on the very right end of the table with my back to the wall; that being the most unnoticeable position available. We all stood until an older gentleman on the far end, cleared his throat and said grace. I had to brace myself to keep my knees from knocking against the chair in front of me. I couldn't help think again how moments of great tension drag by so slowly while pleasure is forever fleeting. Now we all sat, waiting to be served. I smiled, wagering against my own humor that the meal would not be beans and bacon.

Swinging doors separating the kitchen from the dining room began to open. Young girls carrying large plates of food entered, crossed behind the guests and placed the platters on the tables by reaching through and over the shoulders of the seated guests. The girls were adorned in blue and white uniform dresses, crisp and beautiful looking. The most beautiful of them carried a platter to the end of the table and placed it before me saying, "Be careful Sir, it's very hot."

That voice! I looked up at her for the first time. "Julie?"

She stood looking, not saying anything. I thought, "Oh God, it is her. She doesn't recognize me. They have taken her mind!"

Like a falling tree, Julie collapsed against my shoulder, repeating over and over, "Toby, Toby." The spectacle, quite interruptive of a quiet dining atmosphere drew the attention of the wrinkled hair net lady in command of the kitchen.

She emerged in a huff, saying, "What is the world is this?"

With all the guests and servants looking on, neither of us had a quick explanation until I drew from a previous invention.

"My apology ladies and gentlemen, this is my lost sister whom I have been searching for since our parents died."

The comment drew several gasps from around the table, causing the kitchen boss to retort toward Julie, "You never told me this!"

"No mam, it has been too difficult for me to reveal."

Julie looked at me with wonderment in her overflowing eyes.

The kitchen boss said, "My, my, we must get on with supper. Julie, after dinner has been served, you may have the evening off to reunite with your brother. Now let's get on with it."

I don't have any recollection of what I ate. Julie spilled food on a couple of guests, but in good humor they laughed and forgave her.

According to house rules, Julie, a cook's helper, was not allowed to proceed above the first floor of the residence. I waited in the lower parlor until she emerged wearing a regular dress she had obtained from her basement quarters. We walked out into the evening air for privacy, both overjoyed with each other's presence. Merely three paces from the Boarding house, Julie exclaimed, "You must tell me about yourself, BROTHER", with great emphasis on brother.

"I'm sorry, it's all I could think of at that instant."

"I loved it. There is a little chapel just a block from here. We can go in there where it will be warm and we can talk."

Julie led me to a church with a smaller chapel at the side. Candles and oil lamps emitted a warm glow, welcoming us into a quiet corner. She squeezed my hand and said, "You must tell me about yourself. You look so handsome. What have you been doing? Where have you been?"

I protested, "Julie it will take too long. I must hear from you first. I heard from your mother that you were missing, and I feared you were dead."

"My mother?", she squealed, "You heard from my mother? Then it must be true, she is alive."

"She was when I last saw her a couple days after you disappeared."

I decided not to tell her of my encounter with Morgan. I intended never to disclose his demise or his confession. It was my and Wolf's secret, hopefully never to be revealed. I tried again, "Please start from the beginning."

She recounted what I already knew, and I sat quietly while she relived the horror of her separation from her parents. She explained she did not believe Morgan from the beginning, however he forced her into a carriage under the guise of protecting her. During the carriage ride to Roundup he covered her with a blanket saying that she was not safe if Indians or highwaymen discovered her. A year before a small band of Indians had raided their corral and stole several horses, so she thought it possible although not probable. After reaching Roundup, they boarded a stage for Coulson.

With rising emotion, Julie continued the story.

"I told Mean Morgan, that I had an Aunt in Saint Paul where Mother and I visited during the winter. He said he would help me get there. But when we got to Coulson we went to a crummy little hotel where he talked to a man and woman together. I couldn't hear the conversation, but Morgan appeared angry with them. He left cursing, and the woman took me to another building where she said I would have to stay. I told her I wanted to go to my Aunt in Saint Paul, but she said I would have to earn the money for the passage. I asked how I was going to do that, and she didn't give me a good answer, but then said maybe I could work at the laundry."

Julie was shaking with emotion. I put my arm around her and encouraged her to continue. She did, "Soon there were two other girls my same age staying in the same little building. Both of them said they had no parents either and were looking for some way to survive. We agreed to work together in the laundry and look for ways to leave Coulson. The first woman that Morgan talked with seemed to be the boss. She was always giving orders to another one, Wilma White. Wilma was our boss, and was nicer, but we were all afraid of the first one."

"After a couple weeks of washing clothes outside in the cold, they got a young guy to chop wood and tend the fire. "

I broke in, "What was his name?"

"They called him Eddy. Why?"

"I'll tell you later. Please go on."

"Well, Eddy became friends with one of the girls and started to give us ideas about how to get out of Coulson. We had worked for several days, but never got paid. Eddy said they weren't paying us because they wanted to keep us prisoners, and that we would never get out of Coulson."

"The main boss figured out that Eddy was giving us ideas to help us get out of town, and said she was going to get rid of Eddy. But the same day she threatened Eddy, two drunk cowboys came from the saloon and attacked the two girls I was working with. One tore Grace's dress almost off of her. Eddy saw it and went almost crazy. He grabbed a big sharp piece of split wood and clubbed them over the head. The cowboys were hurt bad, but struggled out of sight. Wilma was instructed to get us out of sight before the Deputy Sheriff came because he did not allow young girls to work in town. Wilma hustled the two girls off, but I hung back long enough to hear the boss tell the Sheriff that Eddy started the fight because he was jealous of the cowboys. That was all a lie. She just wanted to get rid of Eddy."

Julie paused to wipe her eyes and continued, "I ran from the laundry yard, but because the deputy was too close by, I went around the front and past the hotel. I was crying and a nice man stopped me as he was coming out of the hotel. He said he was a Magistrate and offered to help. I didn't know what a Magistrate was, but after he explained he offered to assist me and the other girls get as far east as he was going. His destination was Miles City. But he said we had to hurry because the stage was leaving within the hour. I ran to our room and told the other two girls. They agreed to go, but Wilma had not been invited. She broke down saying she wanted to escape too, and confessed she had been paid, and could afford to pay her way to go with us. We all left in a hurry. The Stage was so crowded that the Magistrate had to ride up with the driver until we got to the Ferry at Huntley."

Finally, Julie began to breathe regularly and speak in calmer tones. "We rode for two days. None of us knew what we were going to do when we got to Miles City. The Magistrate said he knew many people there and could get most of us jobs in homes as domestic help. He had associates working for the railroad, and that's how I got here."

She sighed a deep sigh, and said, "The Magistrate promised to contact people he knew in Roundup to learn if my parents were alive. He has not been able to determine for sure. A rancher at the cattle auction related he thought Daddy had been killed, but not by Indians. A horse had kicked him in the chest, and he died of heart failure. They believed Mamma was still alive, but had moved to Saint Paul to be with her sister. I have tried to send telegram notices to Aunt Rosie, but she got remarried and I don't know her new last name or address."

Julie burst into tears again, "I just don't know what I'm going to do."

This was a problem I had no answer for, but I had to console her somehow. I had an idea.

"Tomorrow I'll ask Mr. Lavine. He'll know how to find her."

"Who's he?"

"He's one of the great men who have helped me get where I am."

This time I took her by the hand. "Now I'll give you my story."

It was late when we returned, but the door was still unlocked.

CHAPTER 19 MEETING THE BOSS

Mr. Lavine, came right after breakfast. I had bathed again, just because it felt so good.

His first words were, "Fine, fine, you look just fine."

Pa's hat was lying up on my bed.

Mr. Lavine wasted no time in getting me ready for the meeting. He said, "You will be meeting with the Superintendent of this division, Mr. Hanson. He, along with several others clear back in Saint Paul have read your letter. They were impressed with your skills, but are a little cautious because of your young age. Regardless of your writing skills, they will want to evaluate your personal behavior and people skills. I must say you may fall a little short in the latter category, but I believe you are a quick learner. It may be best to use the same tactic as we did in court. Answer all questions completely, but don't go off telling any long stories. I don't know how big your audience will be, but don't be frightened if there are three or four men staring at you."

I thought, "Oh boy, here we go again. But why should I allow myself to become frightened? At least I am going to have a job. I will be working with smart men who can teach me well beyond the level of Ma and Pa.... well maybe."

The railroad Superintendent was dressed much as I expected; fancy. Not as fancy as Mr. Lavine, but his demeanor stood out from the others.

During introductions I did my best, this time with Ma's ghost on my shoulder. I looked Mr. Hanson in the eye, gave him a strong hand shake and answered with, "Pleased to meet you Sir." My opening statement was, "First I must express how grateful I am to you and your company for the assistance and unexpected attention you have given me. I shall be ever indebted for your kindness."

I saw him look at the other two men in the room and then give a smiling nod to Mr. Lavine. After a few questions and what Pa would have called "small talk" the Superintendent advised, "Toby, what we have in mind for you is more than just taking names at the Coulson station. We have already begun to build a bridge across the Yellowstone near there. We are also going to build an adjacent town, and call it Billings. We are going to need dozens of men because after the bridge is completed, we plan to push all the way through Bozeman by next spring. We should have rails all the way to the west line sometime next summer."

He continued with authority, "We're shipping the tents and cook shack you requested along with a lot of other stuff. Your job will be to make good use of it. I want you to hire good men and help keep them supplied so they stay on. We will pay them out of the Saint Paul Office, but I want you to correctly oversee their payment in the field so neither side gets cheated and we keep the peace. If you need help doing that, we will get you some. Mr. Teel will be busy with the surveying work. As soon as we get things rapidly moving in the right direction, we hope to recognize your talent in different ways that will be better used in our Saint Paul headquarters. But that will be a couple months down the trail. Now do you have any questions?"

"Yes Sir, who do I answer to?"

"Always consult Mr. Teel first, but don't hesitate to telegram me with any problems. Your letters can now reach me in two days. One of the other men here will always be available to assist."

"Thank you, Sir."

"Fine, you can take the work train back tomorrow morning."

Mr. Lavine nodded to me that it was time to exit. I followed him relieved. But before he departed, I had one more question for him. "Sir, how does the railroad find a person when they don't know where they are?"

I explained how important it was for Julie to find her Aunt, and hopefully mother. I pointed out that Julie was actually working for the railroad as an employee of the boarding house.

He smiled and said, "We have an agency that provides that kind of service. Mostly they do guard work, but they should be able to find an old lady. They are called 'Pinkerton.' Would it be appropriate for me to contact Julie directly for any information?"

"Yes Sir, I'll tell her you are working on it."

"Good Toby, consider it done. Now I must go. It has been a pleasure working with you. I look forward to seeing you again, and expect great things from you henceforth."

He turned and walked away, leaving me to find out what time tomorrow my company train left town.

I knew Julie would be working and dared not interrupt her. She needed to support herself at least until her mother could be located, and perhaps beyond.

So much had occurred in the last few days, I walked the streets of Miles City, digesting the experiences and further learning from each exposed store window. I wandered by a very small storefront, which I surmised must be among other things a book store, or perhaps a lending library. Within, I saw on a pedestal, a large open book that at first glance I thought to be a Bible. I touched the pages, only to discover it was a great dictionary. What a thrill it would have been to read from a book this size. Then I remembered that word that drew so much laughter from Eddy. "Prostitute". I thumbed through the pages until I came to the word. I read all three explanations before I understood. Ma always avoided any conversation of a sexual nature. But then I noticed several words on the page I had never seen before. I specifically recall working through the p's although most of the words on each side of the one in question were new to my memory. In front were words like *prosthetics, prosody, prosopography,* and behind were *protagonist* and *protean.* I laughed out loud. Ma, how protective you could be; you removed the page containing the unexplainable prostitute word from the dictionary. During all of my reading of the big book, I never thought to take note of the page numbers. At the time they seemed infinite. Someday I must buy one of the great books for my own.

That evening, Julie and I again talked well into the night. I told her of Mr. Lavine's pledge to elicit the Pinkerton Company to locate her mother. I told her how to find the barrister and assured her she could trust him. We pledged to exchange frequent letters, and I promised to ride the supply train to Miles City at every available opportunity.

We parted that evening with a long hug that developed into a first and forever remembered kiss.

CHAPTER 20   BACK TO WORK

Back at Coulson, I found much had changed. Mr. Teel was pleased to see me return, but anxious to see me relieve the extra burden increased construction activity had placed on him. Additional construction bosses had arrived, most who had been relying on him for organization. He was overwhelmed by the problems of surveying and laying of track and was only irritated with the organization of labor and construction. To the contrary, I loved the excitement of getting people to work and knowing that each day, the big "Iron Horses" were advancing almost two miles further to the west. Most things I organized met with the immediate approval of Mr. Teel in Coulson and Mr. Hanson in Miles City. It gave me confidence to branch out into obtaining support from the Coulson community.

I immediately separated the supervisors into groups by their specialties. New employees were not just posted by name, but were posted to groups such as "railers, spikers, tie setters, graders", and others. I assigned new workers by apparent strength. A few, displaying above average intelligence, I assigned to administrative duties in our office. Before the week ended, I had three additional desks working as payroll clerks, supply clerks and one performing my old job as application clerk. I moved my desk into one of the back rooms. Tents were set up in the town flat in neat rows. Gravel was spread between them to create walkways and the cook shack was to be operating with the arrival of the next supply train. The results were visible in the rising pillars of the river bridge.

Local merchants were reaping the benefits from the increasing railroad population. I was fortunate to obtain salaried employment very quickly upon arrival, allowing me to house myself in a cheap boarding house. However, most others arrived poor and homeless but desperate for work. With my own destitute past fresh in my memory, I promoted an arrangement with local traders. Merchants were willing to extend limited credit to newly hired railroad employees upon verification of employment from my office. I arranged for the employment clerk to verify the amount of wages due to an employee on a certified dated document containing my personal stamp. Thus, an employee could buy on credit, a designated percentage of the stated amount on his document, certified by a "Toby Stamp". The stamp was a disfigured hand stamp I had carved into a barely recognizable TH. When blotted on an ink pad it was almost impossible to forge. The Toby stamp became a well-known and coveted commodity around town. Without the stamp, a newly hired railroad employee without cash, could not obtain credit at the local stores.

Implementation of the credit stamp eventually became complicated. The problem was that the stamp was no guarantee that the worker would pay the merchant, even though he had the money to do so. Merchants had to carefully examine the date of the stamp to preclude the employee using it well after he had spent his wages. Each certification contained the date payment was to be received by the worker, and the expiration date, which was usually three days after payment to the worker. Overall, the policy was quite beneficial to both worker and merchant; allowing the worker to be outfitted on his first day of employment, while the merchant could engage in timely commerce with minimal risk.

Although most workers, after their first pay period did not need the favor of a gracious merchant, there were a few raucous fellows off the range who had little or no experience in handling the generous payments for their work. After a few nights in the saloons and upper floors of the hotels, they were unable to make the payment for which the Toby stamp had vouched for. To protect the credibility of the stamp, under extreme circumstances arrangements were made to withhold wages from employees' payment until the dispute could be settled, almost always by settling the debt in favor of the merchant.

I had never the intent, nor the realization that the Toby Stamp would elevate me to nearly the social economic level of the local banker. But rail workers began treating me with an unusual respect and in worse cases disdain.

With the day's work completed, I was returning to my humble quarters when I was confronted by a pair of rail workers, obviously new to the job; the remains of cow country still on their boots. They had been through our employment office a couple weeks earlier, received the Toby Stamp, and recognized me as the originator of the policy. They were two of the rare cases where wages had been withheld for the proprietor of the general store. Seizing the opportunity of my presence, they both entered into an indignant rage, blaming me as the sole person responsible for their "robber baron" hardship.

My explanation and attempts to reason had no effect on their closed irresponsible minds and the discussion degraded into the larger of the two saying, "I think I ought to just kick your ass."

I had learned much since I was first confronted with that expression and did not present myself in any manner to easily become a victim. I had grown in both body and mind, and wisely recognized there were two of them. I recalled that even Wolf would not attempt to take down two elk at a time. Instead I considered them more vulnerable in the cash side of their pants than their thick skulls would be to a hard pounding.

I responded in a calm voice, "Gentlemen, I am only responsible for you being able to obtain credit ahead of your receiving rail wages payment. I have nothing to do with how you manage money after you receive it. To secure that arrangement with the merchants, I have agreed to assist them in collecting, on a one-time basis per incident, money rightfully owed to them. If you have a dispute, take it up with the merchant. Should you even attempt the ignorant act of kicking my ass, succeed or not, it will be your last effort related to the railroad, and any other job in this town. And lastly if you deem this policy so horrible, I shall, when the sun rises tomorrow, cancel it altogether and notify all who have benefited from it that you two are both responsible for its termination. I'm sure you will find others who will judge not me, but you to be at fault, and who have their own experience and talent in ass kicking."

They both stood there looking at me, saying nothing, as if an interpreter was needed to explain the message. My scolding provided the necessary anesthesia and it was only then I turned my back and strode on down the boardwalk. As I retreated, I remembered the original explanation of Mr. Teel when he counseled me concerning lying about my age. He said it was acceptable if it was for the good of all. The truth was, although I may have been able to get the cowboys fired, I had no influence elsewhere as to their local employment. And I was certainly not about to cancel the credit policy because of two disgruntled failures at finance. However, my comments were for the good. None of us got any bruises or had an encounter with Deputy John. To ease my conscience, I rationalized it as a bluff. Learning this business management stuff was tedious, but I really enjoyed it.

The first few days after my return, I avoided the proximity of the makeshift jail, and definitely Deputy John. I knew that the railroad had considerable political power over John, but disturbing a skunk was never a good idea. However, my journey to the post office required that I pass near the doorway which I usually successfully navigated by going early in the morning. Midday misfortune caused me to almost physically bump into him on the boardwalk. I greeted him with a smile that I hoped wasn't a smirk and said, "Good afternoon Sir."

He grumbled a curt, "I heard you were back in town. I see you sure kissed up to those railroad bosses in Miles City."

I couldn't help it, the response of the Devil made me say, "Yes Sir, and the Judge there liked my teeth too."

I could tell he wanted to slap me flat, but did not do so. When all he did was stand his ground, I sensed I had the advantage. I inquired, "When I last spent the evening in your facility, you seized my rifle for safe keeping. I trust it is still in your care and custody. Because it is a prized possession of my departed father, I would like to reclaim it today."

"Well I'll be damned. You got your nerve."

"Nerve has nothing to do with it Sir. It's my rifle."

"I'll return it to you only if you don't use it anywhere near town, and I don't ever want to see it again, do ya hear?"

I replied to his favor, and we entered the jail. He released the rifle from the same place he had secured it.

Instead of the fright I anticipated from the meeting, I found the mental tug of war rather stimulating and embarked on one more risky venture into John's realm.

"Sir, I have been lamenting about that cowhide from the Circle X. My intention has always been to compensate the Circle X owner for the animal as well as return the hide. I own six cattle remaining in the Musselshell basin, which by telegram, I am going to deed to the Circle X for trade and more than reasonable compensation, to account for the temporary loss from my actions. The railway has now established a freight route within the area that I assume serves the Circle X Ranch. Assuming you have already returned the hide, or are preparing to do so, could you please inform me as to the identity of the Circle X owner and the location where I should send my correspondence?"

He looked at me with hate in his eyes. "You don't own that damned hide!"

By his response he was unavoidably revealing that he had taken personal possession of the hide, or perhaps even sold it himself. The hide was in remarkable shape, cured and would bring a good price.

"Of course, not Sir. I only salvaged it for the rightful owner. I am only asking you as a representative of the law, to guide me to the rightful owner and achieve justice. Now Sir, I must get back to my office. In my absence, Mr. Teel is aware of my desires in this matter and will be happy to assist in the completion of this important mission. Thank you."

I walked away feeling victory, especially since I had already made the arrangements with the Circle X ranch to give them ownership of any and all cattle located on the Hawthorn range and to be compensated for any number more than two. Why did I do it? I'm not sure. Perhaps the child in me was learning the art of human socialization, or should I say the art of getting even. Perhaps it is the art of the Devil. I still have much to learn. I was once punished, causing me to memorize the dictionary. It had immeasurable benefits. Perhaps this small bit of worry would do John some good.

On the return walk to the railroad office I beheld another sight that gave me great satisfaction. I was about to cross the muddy center road of Coulson when I was forced to hesitate by an oncoming horse and rider. The rider, being a handsome cowboy, astride a horse newly appointed with shiny bridle and custom-built saddle was not the distraction. It was the horse. In front of me crossed a large roan gelding, wearing a brand I had seen in the past, showing white socks and a white dot behind his left ear. It definitely was Horse. Someone had found him, claimed him, and made him a proud bearer of respectability.

CHAPTER 21   EDDY

After two weeks progress, I was struggling with a status report which was to be sent to Superintendent Hanson. I was aware of a person approaching my desk when I heard a familiar voice.

"Hi Bub, how ya doin?"

"Eddy, darn your hide. Where did you come from?"

"I came on the wind from Bozeman. That place is crazy. Everybody is heading south looking for gold in the gullies, but it didn't look like there was room or gold enough for me. I hear the railroad was still hiring. Would you know anything about that?"

"Yes, I might know a little about it. But we're moving our office over to the new town called Billings in a couple of weeks as soon as the new building is built. There will be another Sheriff over there that we may get along with a little better. Does John know you are in town?"

"Heck no, but I figure if they let you go, I must be in the clear too."

"I met Julie over in Miles City. She and I have been friends for a long time. She told me what you really did. I owe you some real thanks."

"It wasn't nothing anyone else wouldn't do. Did you run into a girl named Grace over there?"

"Yes, she's there too, and doing fine. They have jobs working in nice homes. If you get on with the railroad you can ride the work train over there."

'Well Bub, how do I get that job?"

"What kind of job do you want?"

"One that pays me millions of dollars every week."

"Now that brings us to another topic. The stolen clothes from the trader down in Huntley. We can't have any theft from the railroad."

"Come on Bub, Jim and I didn't steal nothing from that guy in Huntley. We worked for him for two days pulling the ferry across the river. Come time to pay us he said he didn't have any cash, so we just took a fair amount of clothes with us. He complained, but he was standing right there."

"Where is Jim?"

"He got the gold fever and went south to Virginia City, maybe to Bannack, I don't know. Some guys were headed up to Butte, but mining is not for me."

I asked, "How about herding cows?"

"Look Bub, you know that I ain't no cowboy. I'd rather shovel dirt first."

"I know, but this is different. The railroad will soon be shipping cattle out of Billings and Miles City to the east. They will put them on cattle cars, but it will be a long trip in most cases. We will need stock handlers to water and feed the cattle at rest stops along the way. It will be a good job; much better than hauling rock or wooden ties all day. But if you want to drive rail spikes all the way to California there's a hammer out there just your size."

"H-m-m, all of a sudden I kind'a like the smell of cow poop."

"They tell me you won't even have to sleep with the cows."

"Thank God for that. I thought maybe you were gonna tell me I would have to sleep under one of those cow hides you are so proud of."

"Eddy, I'm done with cow hides. They are too much trouble."

Eddy slapped his leg and we both had a good laugh.

"OK then, we'll get you signed up. Your name still Eddy Kingston?"

"Yup Bub, you got it."

"How do I find Grace?"

"I'll draw you a map."

CHAPTER 22   SAINT PAUL

During most of the organizing activities, Mr. Teel was not interested in the planning and referred me to Mr. Hanson. Communication became a problem. Letters were cumbersome and slow, even when transported by the work train. Mr. Hanson preferred to have meetings often, and required me to travel to Miles City. I enjoyed the process because I always found time to meet with Julie, even if it was only a few hours in the evening at the chapel. She was also extremely busy and had become a leader among her peers, earning a reputation for innovative ways to provide travelers comfort and convenience. We shared time together about twice a month and became closer companions with each visit.

Much of the planning concerning Mr. Hanson centered around the completion of the Northern Pacific Railway. The eastern (westbound) portion was to meet the western, (eastbound) portion at an estimated location west of the continental divide. If predicted schedules were met, the completion date should be in the fall of 1883. A suitable joining location was to be selected and a grand publicity event was being planned to include the attendance of the President of the United States, the President of the Railroad and various other exalted dignitaries.

I had little to do with any of the high-level planning in these meetings. Although my ideas were respected, my age was a handicap placed upon me by the elevated egos of men who had been in the business for many years. I say this not out of disrespect. I recognized my inadequacies and inexperience, but intended to contribute where ever appropriate.

My duties were to record minutes of the meetings and tend to the needs of higher officials within our company. My frequent travels to these meetings made me quite aware of the discomfort of rail travel in the manner to which I had become accustomed. I had become friends with the baggage handler who at one time was my captor in charge of the chain placed around my leg. We had many conversations among the mail sacks and freight, which sometimes was spilling into the passenger compartment. Riding in the baggage car was noisy, dirty, often cramped and generally uncomfortable. Seats in the passenger car were limited and were provided to ticketed customers paying for their passage. I was more or less considered baggage. If one chose to sleep, it was at his own risk, sprawled out over baggage or some other exhausted passenger, too tired to complain.

At one of the meetings devoted to the discussion of attracting high level dignitaries to the completion, or "Golden Spike" celebration, I timidly posed the question of how was the Northern Pacific going to transport and provide creature comforts for persons of high esteem as they crossed the northern wilderness. The room was silent for a moment, causing me to believe I may be admonished for breaking protocol by questioning the high-level planning.

Finally, one of the headquarter officers said, "Well, we have passenger cars, dining cars, and some sleeping cars."

I asked, "What do they look like? Are they suitable for the President of the United States? How many nights will he be required to sleep on the train? If not the train, what hotels would we contract to provide lodging, possibly delaying travel or embarrassing us in route? Gentlemen, I have traveled our train frequently between Coulson and Miles City, and upon my arrival here, have often found it necessary to stop at a suitable place to remove the soil of train travel and make myself respectable for this meeting."

Now it had become really quiet. Mr. Hanson, the executive most familiar with me asked, "Toby, what did you have in mind?"

"Gentleman, this is an excellent time to demonstrate that our railroad is not just a machine to haul cattle to Chicago and coal to Pittsburgh, but also a luxury line to the westernmost points of America. I have jostled many hours in the baggage car, dreaming of riding in a plush coach fit for a president. I have had visions of dining on a fine table of white linen, cutting choice beef with shiny silverware attended by waiters in glossy uniforms. Instead of bouncing across Montana, struggling to sleep stretched upon a canvas bench seat, passengers could be comfortably slumbering in private compartments between laundered sheets. Lounge cars could be coupled at the rear of the train allowing passengers to converse, smoke and sip fine liquor while watching the landscape vanish from their view."

I paused for a breath and to determine the attitude of my audience. The silence provoked me to continue.

"This need not be an enormous effort to begin with. It could start with a few custom-made luxury cars made just for the purpose of the 'Golden Spike' completion celebration. Surely the publicity of it all will prompt important business people to engage in what we can market as 'first class' travel across America, and we can expand the service as demand grows. Someday we might have grand touring coaches with large windows for viewing the grandeur of America."

I finished and looked around for some sort of response. Perhaps it would have been better if I would have left more room for some one of them to claim it was his idea. But it went well.

One of the eastern representatives broke the silence with, "I have been thinking that it would be a good service to begin a luxury passenger service just as Toby described. Perhaps we should initiate the service sooner and apply it to the completion celebration."

The cork was out of the bottle and the Genie had escaped.

Later I was complimented by Mr. Hanson, and asked to elaborate on my vision of a luxury passenger train. I did so with great enthusiasm. He confided that the entire subject was being seriously considered by upper management and that the idea of passenger services could become a significant and separate part of the railroad. He said, "You know, it would be a big change for me. Instead of working to lay railroad ties in the dirt, I could provide for the laying of elbows on dining room tables and heads on pillows."

He concluded by saying, "Thank you Toby. That was a good idea

CHAPTER 23   FINALLY

The Northern Pacific Railway reached Livingston on January 15, 1883. Three months earlier the Pinkerton Company located Julie's mother living with her sister, Julie's aunt Rosie, in Saint Paul, Minnesota. Unfortunately, Julie's father was reported to no longer be living. Julie and her mother were reunited by mail shortly afterward. Julie traveled by rail to Saint Paul for an extended visit with her mother but returned to Miles City upon request of the railroad. The white-haired matron of the boarding house had suddenly become ill. Julie was strongly recruited to the position. She returned to Miles City to manage the boarding house and a little later, take on extra duties of assisting with pullman services for the passenger train. We were pleased that I could continue to travel the rails to spend weekends in Miles City.

The western portion of the railway from Portland, Oregon met the eastern line at Gold Creek, Montana Territory on September 7th 1883. I made the arrangements to have the Northern Pacific President, Mr. Henry Villard, present the golden spike to the dignitaries who drove it in as the last spike. When I say that I made the arrangements I should explain. The golden spike that was the last spike to be driven was not actually made of gold. I painted it a silvery yellow that could be seen by all in attendance.

During the ceremony I was honored to shake the hands of Frederick Billings; the President of the United States, Ulysses S. Grant; and Mr. Villard's relative William Lloyd Garrison.

After the ceremony I was again honored to help serve them in the railroad's special dining car and spoke with Mr. Villard at length on the return trip. He was already aware that I was being credited for having the vision for the plush club car in which we were riding.

Three days after the ceremony, business was not yet returning to normal. The railroad had been built from coast to coast, but several spur lines were planned. Most of the construction crews were being retained but were being required to relocate. I knew that I too was in jeopardy of being moved and reassigned to other duties. Mr. Teel was happy to learn that he would be returning to Miles City.

Shortly after he informed me that he would no longer be my direct supervisor, he returned with a telegram in his hand.

Reading from the message he said, "Toby, you are hereby summoned to the office of Superintendent Hanson at Miles City. Report at your earliest convenience. Report with your personal belongings in preparation for a relocation transfer."

With surging apprehension, I asked Mr. Teel if he knew where I was to be assigned.

His answer was, "Toby it hasn't been discussed with me. You know that we now have offices from Portland to the East Coast. They could move you anywhere. But you don't dare ask because Mr. Hanson, for some reason, wants to tell you himself."

"Isn't that unusual? How did they break the news that you were moving to Miles City?"

"They just sent a letter. There wasn't any urgency to it. I don't know what to tell you. This personal touch could be good, or it could be bad enough that the old boy wants to see you in person and convince you it is a good deal. Toby, you have done an excellent job with us, so don't worry, they aren't going to fire you. And we aren't building railroads in Africa yet, so it can't be too bad."

Mr. Teel knew, but was sensitive enough not to mention the reason for my fear. Julie was still working in Miles City. I did not want to be more than a day's train ride away.

I had few possessions to pack. My wardrobe had grown to a few rough work clothes, my "business" clothes, grooming tools, extra boots, and Pa's hat that I now kept in a box.

I took the night work train to Miles City, this time riding in the rear passenger car. I looked out the back window at the shrinking town of Coulson with both happy and sad feelings. I arrived in Coulson as nothing other than a body with a heartbeat. I had nothing and was in fear of everything. In Coulson, I got my first ever job. I got my first ever "Ass kicking." I slept on the inside of a jail ccll. I became known throughout town for my "Toby Stamp." I made many friends in Coulson, most of whom were staying behind, settling into homes and businesses of their own. The little town was now becoming of lesser importance and Billings was growing into the major town of the area. But it was in Coulson I felt the lowest of emotion, and almost the highest, second only to rediscovering Julie. One just can't leave all of that without remorse, without some part of you being ripped out and left behind. And so it was.

When I reported, Mr. Hanson was brief. He presented me with a letter, and spoke to its subject.

"Toby, I have been promoted to our headquarters in Saint Paul, Minnesota. I'd like you to go with me as my special assistant. If you will accept the position, I suggest we leave next week."

I of course accepted.

I ran all the way to the Northern Pacific boarding house where Julie was working as house manager. I burst into the kitchen, but found it full of workers.

"Julie, come outside, there is something I have to tell you."

CHAPTER 24 CONCLUSION

The ride in the club car was smooth and luxurious. Plush leather and velvet seats were placed in rows beneath curtained windows. Thick carpet dulled the sound of the clicking wheels on steel rails. Lounge tables held food and beverages for those of us fortunate to enjoy the comforts of the single special guest car known as first class.

The *Northern Pacific "Connection"*, an in-house news bulletin circulated throughout the Northern Pacific Company lay on the lounge table of a Glendive cattle baron, traveling east with his aged mother. The cattleman at the request of the distinguished lady began reading the feature article aloud.

"Mr. Henry Villard, President of the Northern Pacific Railroad announced today the promotion of Mr. Lawrence Hanson to director of Marketing Operations and Passenger Services. Mr. Tobias Hawthorn has been promoted as Assistant to that position. Also being promoted within the Services Division is Miss Julie Carlson, to Assistant Director of Pullman services. All three employees will assume their new duties at the N.P. Headquarters Office in St. Paul, Minnesota."

When the cattleman finished reading, his mother looked over at the table where I was sitting and commented, "The world is certainly changing. This train goes to St. Paul. You don't suppose that story is about that cute couple over there?"

I reached over, squeezed Julie's white gloved hand and whispered, "It was wonderful being kids, playing by the creek up along the Musselshell. I will always remember it, but it couldn't last forever."

Julie squeezed back saying, "I know Toby. But you heard the little lady. We are now much more than we used to be."